DEMON & MACHINE

by
Wayne Kyle Spitzer

Being a collection of tales of the machines we live—and sometimes die—by.

It's tempting to say, looking back, that it began with that warped wall—the wall in the basement garage which had been flat and firm when I'd first bought the house but had morphed into something misshapen and hideous. But in truth, it started with her voice, Mia's, a voice I would fall in love with—although, at the time, it existed only in my mind—a voice that had captivated me from the very first moment I heard it.

That would have been March 5, 2019, the day after they'd begun digging for the pool, when I'd taken to the deformed wall (which had been water damaged, I presumed, and was not part of the concrete foundation anyway) with a pickax—hacking away at it mercilessly until both the sheet rock and studs (which had been corrupted, as well) lay in ruins, and I was sitting on an inverted 5-gallon bucket, recovering, just staring at the exposed earth.

At least, until I heard that voice, which said to me, weakly, faintly, and yet somehow clear as a bell, *Please, Dear God. Help me. I have been buried alive.*

It's funny, because the first thing I thought of was a TV movie from the '70s—*The Screaming Woman*, about a girl found buried alive on a rich crone's property, and it's possible I mistook the voice for a memory of that, at least at first. But then it came again (once more managing to be faint yet clear as day), and I realized, finally, that it was not only real but emanating somehow from my own mind, as though I were not so much hearing it as transcoding it into a form I could understand. And what it said was: *Please ... there isn't much time. I'm not far, but as I have awakened, so have they. Now, use your pickax—I won't be hurt—and dig, dig!*

And, because I was captivated, that's what I did, approaching the earthen wall and swinging the ax again and again, grunting each time the blade struck the sediment, feeling the shock in my hands and arms whenever it hit a rock, until at last she cried, *Stop!*—and I stopped, wondering what had come over me that I should throw myself at the stones with such total abandon, or that I should suddenly feel as though I had the strength of twenty men rather than one. At which instant the voice said, *Now, look. See.*

And I did, see that is, and realized that something was glinting, ever so slightly, through the dirt—something metallic, something man-made. Something which revealed itself grudgingly as I dropped the ax and began clearing away the moist, black earth ... until at last I was looking at a State of New York license plate, its blue and yellow colors seemingly vibrant as the day it was pressed, its characters personalized to read: BRN 2 KILL, and its black and white tab dated 3—for March—1966.

As it turned out, we finished our excavations—me and the pool guys—at about the same time; in no small part because they'd lent me their conveyor belt over the weekend, which enabled me to move earth from the garage into the payload of my truck as fast as I could dig it out. Not that I couldn't have managed without it—I felt *strong,* as I said, stronger than I'd felt in years, as if the car and the voice had somehow infused me with super-strength. Nor had my new vitality gone unremarked, especially at Home Depot—which I'd been haunting like a wraith, primarily for support beams—where I was asked more than once what supplements I'd been taking.

Regardless, 48 hours (and several dump loads to my friend's farm) later, it was done, and I was hosing off what a web search had told me was a 1966 Corvette Stingray hardtop, black and red, with a 435-horsepower/5,800 rpm V-8 engine and a sterling Peace symbol—which hung from its rear-view mirror like a charm. Nor was that all, for dangling from its ignition was a set of keys—one, presumably, for the trunk—along with a maroon rabbit's foot, or possibly a cat's, affixed to a silver chain.

Here I pause, in order to better render what I was feeling and what had carried me through the last couple days. For while it is true I began digging (beyond the wall, that is) in response to the girl's cry for help—believing, as I did, that a living person might yet be saved—it is also true that that conviction faltered upon uncovering the 52-year-old plate, to the point that, considering the voice had fallen silent, I no longer expected to find a survivor—but a skeleton. I tell you this plainly so that you will understand why I didn't open the trunk immediately, and why, to be frank, I feared doing so. Rather, I believe it was the car itself that goaded me on during this time, growing as it was in power and actively suppressing Mia's attempts to communicate with me. Whatever it was, she must have at last found a way to break through, for as I opened the driver's side door and seated myself in the cockpit, I once more heard her voice, which said, as clearly as if she were standing next to me: *Hurry. Please. The keys. The trunk ...*

I paused, my fingertips kissing those very keys. The interior smelled of death, and decay, and something else—oily, pungent, like cilantro or burning tires, or a black beetle crushed underfoot. The truth is, I was terrified—what could the voice have been if not the ghost of someone buried with the car? And there was something else too, a completely different reason why I was so hesitant. And that was that—

I closed my thumb and forefingers on the keys, pushing in the clutch.

Don't do it! came the voice. Mia—their specimen. The butterfly they'd intended to collect. *That's what they want; what it wants. What the previous owner gave them. Resist—and open the trunk. We have work to do.*

But I hesitated.

And then came another voice—several others, actually, one after the other—which said, in a language older than words (but which I could understand): *Start it, James ... turn the key.*

Yes, yes, James. Continue the process.

Do it, James!

And I turned the key.

The truth was, I hadn't noticed how much attention my little digging project had garnered until I backed the rumbling, sputtering 'Vette up and out of the garage—and found half the neighborhood looking on. I shouldn't have been surprised; there were piles of dirt and stone everywhere—some of which had spilled onto the Merton's lawn (and the Diller's, too) and made tempting obstacles for boys on BMX bikes, not to mention that the conveyor running at 3 am would have undoubtedly stirred Miss Harper, who had once called 911 because a dog was barking. It's hard to credit, in retrospect, how I'd avoided a visit from the cops. Maybe *they* had something to do with it. The bugs. Who knows.

Regardless, the kids waved and hollered as I backed onto the street and put it into gear, and I gave them a rev or two before easing up on the clutch and moving down the road, the radio giving me a start as it came on without warning (and without my having touched it) and began playing "Fortunate Son" by Creedence Clearwater Revival.

Then I was off, cruising the streets of Schenectady as though I hadn't a care in the world, relishing it every time I drew alongside some kid in his Honda, speeding up a little as I handled corners, tapping the horn as I rumbled past female joggers. The truth of it is I was under the car's spell, and didn't think to question why the girl had fallen silent (again) or who—what—the other voices had been or how a car that had been buried for 52 years had simply rolled over and leapt to life. I felt young again, vibrant, strong, as though nothing could touch me and nothing could hurt; as though the logical part of my brain had simply turned off, as it does when you smoke a good blunt; as though I were in the clouds and nothing could bring me back. Indeed, I felt free of all human constraint and concern—at least, until I saw the Lyndon B. Johnson campaign sticker on the clean, chrome bumper ahead of me, and, realizing that both it and the Beetle to which it was attached were in as perfect condition as the 'Vette—"Black Betty" it said on the 'Vette's door, I'd nearly forgotten about that—began to come out of it.

That's when I really noticed it, the fact that the landscape immediately around the car had changed; that it had—*reverted,* somehow. I can only describe what I saw, which was that *none* of the vehicles at the light could have been newer than a '66, and that the *light* itself looked decidedly retro, decidedly quaint, at least compared to the one only a block away. More, the storefronts alongside had changed, so that a Kinney Shoe Store now stood where a Taco Bell had just been, and a Woolworth had replaced an Indy Food Mart. Likewise, the pedestrians had changed—yoga pants giving way to miniskirts, athletic shoes giving way to go-go boots and winklepickers, short hair giving way to long. And it was as I observed these things that I noticed something else—the Stingray's reflection in the Woolworth's front windows, or rather, the reflection of something which was not the Stingray but which stood—hovered—in its place: a long, translucent, green-black thing, like an enormous wine decanter, only laid on its side, which glowed slightly from within its bulbous body and seemed to warp the very air around it, to bend it, to curl it like burnt paper.

What you see is the car's true form, came the voice, the girl's voice, Mia's, startling me with its clarity, seeming at once to be both inside my head and without, causing me to turn instinctively— revealing her to be sitting beside me, right there in the passenger seat. *"... and the field in which it operates. That field is weak now but it will grow. And the longer it remains free—the car, the artifact—the stronger it will become, until the world itself becomes threatened. Now do you see why I tried to warn you?"*

But I could only stare at her, even as the late afternoon sun caught her auburn hair—which was styled in a flipped bob—and seemed to set it on fire. *Beautiful,* I remember thinking, even though her eyes and skin were all wrong: bluish-gray, almost green; deaden, but in a very specific way, as though she had drown. "Look at yourself," she said (actually said, it seemed, not communicated silently, like a specter), "Although its passengers are immune to the field it has already affected you—in other ways."

I adjusted the rearview mirror to look at myself, and saw that she was at least partially correct: my skin was sallow—almost greenish—and there were dark spots beneath—

That's when I saw them. *The bugs.* Three of them, to be precise, scrunched up in the storage area beneath the fastback, each about the size of a chimpanzee, and each a kind of hybrid between a locust and a mantid.

It was all too much—the car that had been buried for 52 years yet started right up, the flashback to the 1960s and the ghostly girl, the bugs the size of dogs whose stench filled the cab and caused me to wretch. I gripped the door handle instantly—even as the little chrome knob dropped, locking me in. Then we were accelerating— abruptly, powerfully—whipping around the cars in front of us and blasting through the intersection: the girl vanishing, just winking out of existence, the bugs making a sound like crickets but magnified a hundred fold—the V-8 (or whatever it was) roaring.

Yes—yes, James. Want this, we do ...

Want it! Want it!

Right there, James. The infestation. Do it!

But I wasn't driving—

No, I could see that wasn't true: my foot was on the peddle just as sure as my hands were on the wheel. And that foot dipped suddenly even as the skateboarder came into view—his eyes widening, his free leg kicking—so that he disappeared into an alley even as we exploded past—fishtailing to a halt in the middle of the road, where the high-compression engine sputtered and the glass packs rumbled—before my foot once again hit the gas and we tore after him, burning rubber.

And then we were bearing down upon the kid, as he kicked and kicked furiously and glanced at us over his shoulder. As I looked in the rear-view mirror and saw the bug-things leaning forward (as though in anticipation). As I fought whatever impulse had taken oven my limbs and partially succeeded—too late.

There was a *thud-crunch!* as he vanished beneath the hood—and the car bucked violently, as though I'd driven over a curb. I ground the brakes, glancing in the mirror—saw him tumble after us like a bag of litter. Only then, after I'd come to a complete stop, did it occur to me: I could see out the back window. The bugs were gone. The kid, meanwhile, was still alive—good God!—and thus it wasn't too late; I could still help him, still *save* him.

Yes, yes, James. Save him.

We're not finished yet, James.

Finish, finish!

I felt the gearshift in my hand—saw that I'd already put it in reverse and was stepping on the gas, letting out the clutch. And then the car launched backward—reversing straight as an arrow—until it bucked and rolled up onto the kid; and stopped.

"Please, mister," came the kid's voice—muffled, garbled—through my partially open window. "Please, God—"

But then my hand was shifting and the engine was roaring—the wide tires were spinning—and I saw through my side-view mirror that his blood was fanning the nearby bricks and a window—spraying them like rifle shot, spattering them with entrails, hurling pieces of bone against, and through, the glass—until the positraction gripped bare asphalt and the car leapt forward: roaring down the alley, skidding back onto the road, releasing its control over me.

At which moment Mia reappeared, like an apparition, and, rolling her milky eyes to face me, said, "Now will you listen? Now will you open the trunk?"

And then promptly faded away.

The key slid in smoothly and I paused, looking at the abandoned drive-in theater: at the rusted, canted speaker posts (the speakers themselves had long since been stolen) and the weeds bursting through the concrete berms; at the dilapidated concessions bar and the partially-collapsed steel fence. *Do it,* I told myself, and turned the key, hearing sirens in the distance as the trunk popped open, trying not to think about the kid. As it turned out, it wasn't that difficult, considering what I found myself looking at.

They were arthropods, of course, and so appeared in death much as they'd appeared in life, although their eyes had long since rotted out and their shells had become gray as tombstones. But that's not what interested me so much as what was beneath them—which, having shoved them all to one side, I realized was a kind of—well, *egg,* for lack of a better term. A huge, glass egg—built into the car and full of a greenish, glowing liquid—within which, curled into a fetal position, floated a naked woman. A woman I recognized as Mia her-self.

Now do you understand? she asked, speaking directly into my head, directly into my mind—again, as though she were standing immediately beside me.

"No. No, I don't," I said, shaking my head in the dimming twilight. "Maybe you can explain it to me."

Get in the car, she said. *And I will. All of it.*

That's when I looked over the trunk lid I saw that she was back, just sitting in the passenger seat like a zombie, staring straight ahead at the screen. A screen, I might add, which had been restored—and over which danced images of hot dogs and fountain sodas and fresh-popped corn; of cotton candy and licorice twists.

For the drive-in, you see, had *warped*—just like the streetlight, just like the storefronts—and was operational once again. Operational and rapidly filling up—with cars, that was a given, old yet somehow brand-new—but also with people, at least some of whom would have been dead, or so it seemed likely to me, only a few scant moments ago.

"Talk," I said, shutting my door, settling in. "Starting with why you encouraged me to unbury the car—when you knew full well what could happen." I glanced at her in the dark. "And you *must* have known."

"I knew that their spirits—which are fused with the car, as is mine—would attempt to influence you, yes. What I did not know is the extent to which they'd succeed, how easily you'd succumb!" She seemed to shift gears: "It's not important. What is important is that the car gets reburied—deeper, further away. So that it may never threaten the surface again."

"But, what is it ... and who are they? Who are you, for that matter?"

"The car? Why, it's a spacecraft, of course. A *time*-craft. It has been matter-cloaked to mimic an automobile, that's all—of a make and model that was popular in the year they came. It was their way, I suppose, the bugs, of moving amongst us; of observing us at close range—at least, until they decided we should be exterminated. That's where I come in: their specimen. The sole butterfly they'd planned to harvest as an example of what they'd wiped out—for that's precisely what they'd initiated before a flu strain killed them all."

She laughed suddenly and what looked like the green fluid from the egg gurgled up out of her mouth. "The Common Cold, I suppose. Like in H.G. Wells. At least that's what Crowley thought, when he found them, that is."

"Who—"

"Crowley, the man who first discovered the car, full of bugs and rolled over in a ravine near Schenectady, in 1966. It was his theory that the foreigners had taken the appearance of humans while piloting the cloaked craft, but reverted to bugs after they'd died—either way, he knew right away that the 'Vette was no mere car. As for me and my egg, he hadn't a clue what to make of that. But the bugs spoke to him just as they've spoken to you; and before he knew it he'd stuffed them in the trunk and towed the car home and applied for title—he even had a personalized license plate made, 'BRN 2 KILL,' something to do with his service in Vietnam—as well as commissioning someone to paint 'Black Betty' on its door. But by November of that year he was done, and wanted nothing further to do with it, even going so far as to bury it in the landfill he worked at, the Copperhead Earth Works, where he plowed it 6 feet under with his bulldozer and—"

"Copperhead?" I interjected, and thought instantly of Copperhead Farms, the name of the housing project which encompassed my new home. "How do you know all this?"

"I began to, project myself—sleepwalking, I call it—shortly after being preserved in the back of the ship. Nor do I know how that is possible. I only know that it is, and that I was able to monitor Crowley as he interacted with the car—although I could not yet communicate with him as I have with you. And it was during that time that I became aware of *them,* the bugs, but in spirit-form. I even learned how to intercept their thoughts, as I had Crowley's. All of which brings me to why I reached out to you when you began to dig—"

"You wanted to be free," I said, feeling as though I suddenly understood her, suddenly got it. "Either by death or by rescue ... you wanted to be free."

"In part, yes. Of course. But also because the car was insufficiently buried, insufficiently interred. It was bleeding through the sediment, you understand. Because what the bugs started before falling ill is still underway—an exponential charge, using the ship's warp field as a weapon of mass destruction. And as I've said, the longer the car remains free, the stronger it will become ... until at last all life on Earth will be threatened. And before you ask, the answer is no, it cannot be destroyed, not without detonating it at its present charge, which would still be enough to destroy half the planet."

I moved to speak but paused, letting it go.

"That's what I meant when I said we had work to do. We *have* to find a way to re-bury this car. And re-bury it for good. And for that you're going to need help—real help, not a disembodied voice. Or a ghost. And so I am asking you to at least try to set me free. But in order to do so you'll have to *see,* and I mean see in a way you've never seen before. I'll show you. I—I have faith in you, James. I know you can do it."

And then she placed her hand over mine and it faded into my skin, and I got out and went to the trunk.

I'd just told her that, because of her help, I could see—actually *see* the alien-looking control panel (which before I'd missed), when a youthful male voice said, behind me: "Excuse me, sir?" —and I spun around.

What is it, James? What's going on?

And found myself facing a security guard—one right out of 1960s—peaked hat, whistle, Billy club, and all.

"Y—yes?" I stammered, easing down the trunk lid, stepping away from the car. "Can I help you?"

He aimed his flashlight, a ribbed, chrome thing which looked positively primitive, into the empty cab.

"It's just funny," he said, "because I could have sworn I heard you talking to someone—in the trunk of your car. Just now, as I was coming up the aisle."

He paused, sizing me up. "You know, a lot of people seem to think that ripping us off by sneaking people in through the trunk is just good, clean fun." He unhooked the radio from his belt and placed it near his lips. "But 3.50 a carload means just that—*3.50 per carload.*" He keyed his mic. "K-91 to K-54, where are you?"

"Look, can't we just—"

Get in the car, James.

"I mean, I'm a little old to be sneaking—"

Get in the car, James!

"Stay right where you are, sir. K-91 to K-54: Request back-up in section A. *Excuse me, sir ...!*"

But I was already getting in the car, turning the ignition—revving the engine as Barney Fife rushed to my door and began yanking the handle—which I'd locked—putting it in gear.

"Get us out of here," said Mia, having re-appeared in the passenger seat. *"Go, go, go!"*

And then we'd backed up and swung around and were beginning to launch forward, the 'Vette's engine roaring, its rear tires spinning, until we blasted between the rows and I began searching for the exit, the skinny guard gradually giving up the chase, people running helter and skelter out of our way.

Yes, yes, James! Infestation!

Kill them, kill them!

Wipe them from the Earth ...

The bugs again—reaching into my mind, seizing control of my hands—as the radio sputtered to life and the Beatles began singing: *Well, shake it up, baby, now (Twist and shout)*

Come on, come on, come on, baby, now (Come on and work it on out ...)

My hands jerked the wheel as a man in a suit ran out in front of us and we struck him like a hammer—causing him to tumble up over the hood, splay against the windshield, where his bloodied face pressed against the glass. *Well, work it on out, honey ...* The wipers activated even as I slammed on the brakes and he slid off, then we were accelerating again, rolling over the top of him, as Mia screamed and the bugs ticked and cackled, as the Beatles sang, *You know you got me goin' now (Just like I knew you would ...)*

"Fight it, James! Resist them!" cried Mia—even as the car bounced up and over a berm and the Peace symbol hanging from its mirror swung. As it targeted a woman with an enormous beehive and rammed into her at full speed—knocking her at least twenty feet, trampling over the top of her, leaving her a bloody ruin.

"Get it together, man! Concen—oh, no. *Oh, no!*"

I followed her gaze as we fishtailed around the end of the front row and accelerated toward the screen, saw the children begin to scatter as we bore down upon the playground.

Do it, James, do it!

Faster, faster!

I fought the wheel but it had taken over completely—steering for the running kids, seeming almost to growl at me, jerking against my grip. The cab shook as we piled over the railroad ties at the edge of the playground and began tearing through the sand, aiming at a little boy even as the headlights popped up and drowned him in harsh light, as the glass packs roared and the Peace symbol swung.

"James!"

And something just—kicked in. I still can't explain it. But for a fraction of a second I was able to just, *merge* with the car—with the ship. All I know is that for that fraction of a second we were one: one entity, one organism. And as I applied the brakes and swung the wheel the car responded, fishtailing and skidding to a stop in the sand ... where it idled roughly as I looked at Mia and she looked at me. And it was at precisely that moment that an idea came to mind—an idea I thought just might work. If we could get there in time. If I could maintain control of the car.

It wasn't easy, communicating with the car, ordering it to lower its warp field; nor was it completely successful—the family we'd left twisted and mutated at a stoplight, partially fused with their car, was proof of that. Nor did we stop anymore after that but instead rumbled straight for my house, ignoring every sign and limit, rushing against the clock, praying we could make it before my concentration finally gave out and we were back in the '60s—back where we'd killed so many and the cops were surely looking for us. Back where the bodies lay scattered and broken everywhere we'd been.

"Hang on!" I shouted as we broke through the fence and hurtled toward the pool excavation—forgetting, for the moment, that Mia was yet a kind of ghost, and that if anyone need worry about the coming impact it was me. And then I was throwing open the door and rolling upon the ground—as the 'Vette which was not a 'Vette launched off a dirt berm (left over from the pool dig) and crashed into the pit, its steel frame seeming to howl like a wounded beast and its fiberglass crunching and breaking, its windows shattering ...

Hurry, James. The cement truck ...

"But you're still in the car!"

And it's possible I'll remain there. The world, James ... The world comes first.

I cursed, staring into the pit. At the Stingray, which had begun to glow and to morph. At *Black Betty* ... a bitch if ever there was one. Then I hurried to the cement truck and, to my great relief, found the keys still in the ignition (we'd become friends, after all, the contractor and I, nor was it a bad neighborhood). But I was not alone as I started it up and activated the mixer, for in addition to Mia the bugs were still in my head, louder than ever and seeming to sense what was at stake. *Angry,* for that was their nature, but terrified, too. Vulnerable at last.

Don't do it, James. You mustn't do it ...

Return, return. Drive us some more.

The girl, James. You must save the girl!

I looked at the pit as it began to fill up with concrete, frowning, then scrambled from the truck and into the hole, my shoes squelching in the cement, my heart racing, as I opened the door and retrieved the keys. As I hurried to the trunk and popped it open.

But the alien control panel was no longer there, which is to say I could no longer see it given the maelstrom in my head, the energy I was expending to thwart the ship's warp field. And it *was* becoming a ship again, that much was clear, as though the bugs' fear and vulnerability had weakened it and compromised its ability to multitask. As though their hatred of us and of the human race had trumped every other single thing. The charge had to be perpetuated; I could practically hear it in the air. The purge had to continue—even if it was from beyond their own graves!

And then a miracle occurred, one Mia and I talk about to this very day, although really it was just the result of the green-black ship losing its bizarre cloak: for as the wet cement reached my knees and threatened to overwhelm the trunk, the control panel reappeared, at which instant I was able to access the bugs' minds—for Mia's abilities had rubbed off on me in a way we still don't understand—enough to depress the right sequence and cause the egg to open, its greenish fluid flooding the ship's surface as Mia inhaled violently and coughed up yet more liquid—the bugs chattering and cursing indecipherably as the concrete reached for my thighs. And then, somehow, somehow, I was able to scoop her into my arms and climb out of the pit, although, again, the fact that I was able to do so remains a mystery to us even today. Perhaps it was just love and the power it can confer. For I *did* love her, of that much I was certain. And I wasn't about to abandon her to another eternal limbo.

All I know is that at some point the pit had been filled and I'd successfully shut down the mixer, and that we'd stood there for what seemed a long time just watching the cement cure and feeling grateful for our lives. Nor was it a time for celebration considering how much pain and suffering the thing had caused; but rather a time to reflect and meditate and yes, to pray.

Pray that no one ever came and dug the cursed thing out.

Pray that the bugs, whatever they were and wherever they were from, would never send another.

VORPAL

Statement of Mrs. Casey Marie Dunn (March 5ᵗʰ, 9:30 AM, interviewed by Detective Lamar Shaw)

Detective Shaw: Okay, now, I want you to focus, and tell me exactly what happened—starting with the landing of the canoe. Can you do that for me?

Dunn: Sure—yeah, I think. (sniffling) I ... we were taking on water, like I said. Not enough to sink—I'm not sure you can sink a canoe, can you? But enough so that we'd become extremely uncomfortable, and wanted to know where it was coming from.

Detective Shaw: So you landed the canoe near the Pyreridge Wind Farm. To inspect it.

Dunn: Yes. Well, we didn't know about the wind farm, not yet. There was only a thin width of beach—or whatever you'd call it—before the cliffs, which climbed straight up and sort of plateaued—and that's where the turbines were, still out of sight.

Detective Shaw: Out of earshot, too?

Dunn: You know, it's funny you should ask me that. I mean, yes—but ... but no, too. Because I remember sensing— a kind of pressure—like, like something heavy was laying on the air itself. Like, you know that feeling you get when you go up in elevation and your ears need to pop? —like that, only softer, more elusive. I honestly thought I was imagining it—at least until Bobby turned the boat over and we saw the hole in its bottom, at which the pressure seemed to increase (to double, actually), though only for a moment. Then it subsided and we were just standing there, looking at that hole. That funny little hole.

Detective Shaw: That's a curious way to describe it ... 'that funny little hole.' Was there something unusual about it?

Dunn: Well—yes. I should say so.

Detective Shaw: What? What was so unusual?

Dunn: It—it was shaped like a spiral. A perfect, proportionate little spiral, just as smooth and perfect as if it had been molded into the boat.

Detective Shaw: You mean drilled into the boat, surely?

Dunn: No. I mean molded. Or—I don't know—melted, maybe. But definitely not drilled.

Detective Shaw: And you'd never noticed it before?

Dunn: No, of course not. If that were the case, we'd never have embarked on the trip—much less without our phones.

Detective Shaw: Yes, I've been wondering about that. Help me understand, could you? It seems irresponsible to have left without them, even on such a wide, lazy river. Weren't you concerned about, say, an unexpected weather event? Or having a medical emergency? Being doctors, I can't imagine that—

Dunn: Mr. Shaw, please. You have to understand, the on-call nature of our jobs was precisely why such an excursion had become necessary in the first place. Surely it's the same in police work? No, this once, for our sanity and for our marriage, we were going commando, as they say. No cellphones, no iPads, no anything but nature and each other for the duration of the trip. That—at least that much makes sense ... doesn't it?

Detective Shaw: Of course, Mrs. Dunn. I suppose it does. But, my God, being so far from the nearest town, and not even knowing precisely where you were at, that must have been terrifying. What on earth did you plan to do?

Dunn: Well, the only thing we could do, which was to right the boat and continue on—while doing our best to bail, of course. And that's when I first noticed it: way up there beyond the ridge; something moving, swinging, like the tip of a giant sword—only black against the sun—something which, after we'd scaled a nearby rockfall, turned out to be the blades of an industrial wind turbine—just one out of what seemed an endless array, spread out across the scrublands for as far as the eye could see, casting long shadows, like Cyclopean sentinels.

Detective Shaw: Cyclop—cyclopean—what is that? Is that Latin?

Dunn: Huge, Detective. Massive.

Detective Shaw: Right. And then, what? You returned to your boat?

Dunn: You know we didn't return to the boat.

Detective Shaw: Yes, I understand that, just as I understood they found a spiraled hole exactly one inch in diameter in the bottom of your canoe. But it's better for the record if I pretend I know nothing, okay?

Dunn: Okay. No, then we began walking, because we'd figured out where we were at—the Pyreridge Wind Farm just north of Edgerton, as you said. And we knew, also, that they gave tours there and even had a visitor's center; a center which might still be staffed even though it was extremely late in the day, and which would have a telephone.

Detective Shaw: A wise move.

Dunn: Yes, it was as good as any. Or so it seemed—until we came to the wind turbine with the white service truck parked at its base; and saw ... where we saw ...

Detective Shaw: Yes?

Dunn: You've seen the pictures, Detective.

Detective Shaw: But I need to pretend I have not. And I need to hear what you, personally, saw with your very own eyes. For the record, Dr. Dunn. Please.

Dunn: Where we saw a man, a service technician, by his clothes, hung by his neck from his own safety line ... from the back of the wind turbine's nacelle. Just ... just sort of swaying there, in the wind. A man who was missing one shoe. And who ...

Detective Shaw: Go on ...

Dunn: And who had no discernible face. Okay? (inaudible) He had no face. Isn't that good enough?

Detective Shaw: I didn't mean to upset you. Still, talk about that a little. You say, 'he had no face'—what does that mean? Had it been mutilated or disfigured in some way? Was he wearing a nylon? What?

Dunn: No, no, nothing like that. It was just, dark, somehow. Smudged out. The truth is we couldn't tell; it was like the whole world was in focus except for that one spot, which was blurred, unlit. That's when I noticed all the little holes in in the truck, like it had been riddled with bullets— except on closer inspection they turned out to be spirals, like the one in the boat. I say 'I' because Bobby's attention had drifted to the blades of the wind turbine, which were directly above us, going woosh, woosh, woosh. And it was the strangest thing because it was almost as if he'd become hypnotized—as if they were a great swinging pendulum—to the point that he completely ignored me when I pointed out the visitor's center and only continued to watch.

Detective Shaw: Well, that is strange. Was he in shock, you think?

Dunn: My husband? The emergency room doctor? (laughter) No. No, this was something—different. Something more meditative. Almost as if—

Detective Shaw: Something spiritual?

Dunn: Yes! As though he were having an epiphany. To the extent that I had to physically drag him away; at which he came out of it and was just Bobby again—just everyone's favorite life-saver.

Detective Shaw: And that's when you went to the visitor's center and called the police.

Dunn: Yes. It—it was unlocked. We just walked right in. But no one was there, even though there was a utility truck out front. And then I called the police but the dispatcher had bad news: they wouldn't be able to get there for a half-hour, at least. And that's when I just, well, broke, for lack of a better term, and the next thing I knew I was waking up while Bobby dabbed at my temples with a moist cloth and the phone rang incessantly and he began telling me to answer it, that it was 911 calling back, and that he'd searched for the keys to the truck out front but hadn't found them and was going to go back to the first truck—the truck with all the holes in it—to see if its keys were there.

Detective Shaw: And how did you feel about that? About him returning to the scene? Or you being left alone in the visitor's center, for that matter?

Dunn: Oh, I thought it was a terrible idea! I didn't want to let him out of my sight. There was something so strange about him all of a sudden— so out of character—like he was high on marijuana. And his eyes, they were so distant, so unfocused. I practically begged him not to go. But then he had gone and I was answering the phone, and the dispatcher kept me busy with questions for I don't know how long ...

Detective Shaw: You say he wasn't himself and that his eyes were blurry; was there anything else? Was his speech slurred, for example? How about his color?

Dunn: He—he kept scratching himself, like he was covered in insect bites. And he was pulling at his clothes, especially his collar, as though they were suffocating him. It was all so very unusual, and I would have dropped the phone and ran after him if not for ... if not ...

Detective Shaw: If not for what, Dr. Dunn?

Dunn: If not ... for the blood. The blood on the glass case.

Detective Shaw: I'm afraid I don't—

Dunn: Stop. Just, stop, please. You know as well as I do that—

Detective Shaw: But the tape recorder doesn't, Mrs. Dunn. Now, please. Tell me what you saw that prevented you from pursuing your husband. Describe it to me.

Dunn: There—there was a large glass case in the center of the foyer ... it ... it contained a miniature of the wind farm., as you know. And it—someone had written something on top of it. Some kind of a message. In blood.

Detective Shaw: I see. Thank you. Now tell me: what did this message say?

Dunn: It ... I don't remember exactly. It was mostly gibberish. Something about 'the Wind' and 'the Way,' and going in to 'Them.' Something about how 'They' had attached themselves to the turbines—whatever 'They' were. And finally just a long scrawl, followed by a warning, all in caps, GET OUT OF HERE AS FAST AS YOU CAN.

Detective Shaw: I see. And I guess it needs to be asked: Did you? Or did you continue to field the 911 operator's questions?

Dunn: No. I dropped the phone as fast as I could and ran out the side door, the one Bobby had went out. And the first thing I saw was Bobby's pale-blue windbreaker, just thrown aside in the dirt, and further out, his T-shirt, white against the sage.

Detective Shaw: It's like he was burning up. Was it hot out? What was the temperature, you think?

Dunn: It was cold! No, like I said, it was if the clothes were suffocating him, cutting off his circulation. All I know it that when I reached the T-shirt I saw his belt further out, and beyond that, his shoes, just lying amidst the cheat-grass. That's when I knew something truly terrible had happened, was happening, and that if I didn't find him quickly he might genuinely hurt himself; though I'd scarcely had the thought when I noticed someone crumpled face down in the sage—not Bobby, this man was fully dressed—and ran to him.

Detective Shaw: The other turbine technician.

Dunn: Oh, are we done with the ignorant act?

Detective Shaw: It was a slip; I'm starting to think about lunch. Okay, and, seeing this, what did you do?

Dunn: He wasn't breathing and so I rolled him over. And ...

Detective Shaw: Yes? And what?

Dunn: Jesus, gods, you know what!

Detective Shaw: What did you see when you rolled him over, Dr. Dunn?

Dunn: I saw that he had no face. That it ... that it had just spiraled in, like the hole in the boat. That there was a gaping funnel where his eyes and nose and upper lip should have been—mottled red and black, pink and gray—just twisted cartilage and brain tissue. And then his body spasmed, as though by a reflex, and the funnel seemed to burp, spitting up blood.

Detective Shaw: Jesus.

Dunn: After which, dear God, I can't say, because I was running away as fast as I could; past Bobby's shoes and toward the wind turbine (the one with the truck parked at its base), as well as past a few dozen new funnels in the ground—which grew in size as I approached from an inch or two across to ones the size of manhole covers. Until I came to the turbine and—and stopped dead in my tracks. Because there was Bobby kneeling prone in the dirt, like a Muslim, I suppose, or a Buddhist, but completely nude—bowing before the turbine, the hatch of which was open, seeming almost to pray.

Detective Shaw: But ... but all right, in spite of his behavior.

Dunn: No, Mr. Shaw, not 'all right.' Because when he sat up again I saw that his back was ... It was riddled with those same spiral funnels. There were even some in his arms. But—but that wasn't all. Because, after he'd stood with some difficulty and turned to face me (he must have sensed my presence; that or saw my shadow), I realized something else. And that was that his eyes had gone completely white—rather they had rolled back in his skull enough so that only the whites were visible—at which moment he spoke and said, calmly, "The turbines, don't look at them. They eat your eyes."

Detective Shaw: The turbines ... they ... what did that mean?

Dunn: I'm sure I don't know. All I know is that my husband had become something hardly recognizable ... and that I was terrified. So much so that I began backing away as he approached— which seemed to anger him, enough that when he resumed speaking he sounded vicious—alien—full of disdain.

Detective Shaw: Good lord—what did he say? Think, Mrs. Dunn. This is the most vital part of your testimony ...

Dunn: He said that he was taking the way of the wind and the sky, and that he was going in—to Them—by which I presume he meant going into the tower and scaling the ladder. And he said other things: That our thoughts made patterns in their world—left 'prints,' as it were—as did theirs in ours; and that that was how they'd found us, by listening to our thoughts, zeroing in on our patterns. And he said that Bobby was merely a bundle of sensory organs wrapped in a skin of decaying matter and so wasn't important, wasn't needed. That only they mattered—they, the beings attached to and inhabiting the turbines. And that ... that ...

Detective Shaw: What, Mrs. Dunn? Say it.

Dunn: But ... don't you see? It doesn't matter what he said, because it wasn't him speaking, not really. Bobby would never have described a human being as just a bundle of sensory organs; he truly believed, with every fiber of his being, that we were more than that—more than just the sum of our parts—it was what inspired him to become a doctor in the first place. And knowing what I knew, knowing what kind of man he was, I pressed him, telling him that Bobby did matter—that he mattered to his patients and that he mattered to me—more than I would ever be able to describe. And then I approached him and embraced him and told him I loved him—feeling, for the briefest of moments, the spirals beginning to close on his back—and he smiled, his eyes returning to normal, after which he said, or started to say, "I love ..." (room tone)

Detective Shaw: (inaudible) He—he told you he loved you?

Dunn: No. He ... his eyes rolled back ... and then his face, it ... it simply imploded. In a spiral. Like someone had flushed a toilet full of blood and brains.

(room tone)

Dunn: And then his body, which had become light as a feather, like a papery husk, came apart in my arms—and simply blew away. Like so many dandelion seeds.

(room tone)

Detective Shaw: I ... I have to ask. It's—it's my job, you understand. Did—did you ever feel like ... I mean, did—

Dunn: Did I ever feel like I was being targeted myself?

Detective Shaw: (inaudible)

Dunn: Yes, right after that. I'd—I'd turned my palms up, see, because I couldn't comprehend that he could be there one minute and just ... gone the next. And there were spirals in both of them. Not deep, just, just impressions, but it was enough to snap me out of whatever I was feeling and to open the door of the truck, where I found its keys right there in the ignition.

Detective Shaw: And that's when you drove onto the highway and—

Dunn: And didn't stop until I reached Edgerton. Not even when the squad cars started passing me going the other way, their lights flashing.

Detective Shaw: Yes, well. When they got there they found things much as you described ... and photographs were taken. The other men, the turbine technicians, they ... when we tried to move them they, too, were lost to the wind.

Dunn: And the turbines? Have they been inspected?

Detective Shaw: (inaudible) Just turbines. Nor has there been any reports of ... strange occurrences. It would seem, then ... that this was an isolated event.

Dunn: An isolated event ...

Detective Shaw: Yeah.

Dunn: Are—are we done, Mr. Shaw?

Detective Shaw: Yeah. For now. There's ... there's a car downstairs; they'll, ah, take you home.

(inaudible shuffling)

Detective Shaw: Oh, and Mrs. Dunn? Thank you. I know ... it couldn't have been easy.

Dunn: Goodnight, Detective.

Detective Shaw: Goodnight.

(end of recording)

GOLEM

Why did I do it? *Because I was meant to.* Because that's why I had been allowed to live. This was the whole of the affair in one simple statement.

Memory, of course, can be a dodgy thing: why else would my recall of the Benton Boys—and how Old Man Moss had brought their reign of terror to an end—have lain dormant for so long (forty years, to be exact), right up until that moment I saw what I'd at first taken to be a man—but quickly realized was not—ascending the tower crane just beyond our encampment?

The obvious answer is that a lot can happen in forty years. A man could go from being an innocent kid in Benton, Washington (population one-hundred and seventeen) to a scary homeless dude in Seattle—Belltown, to be precise—just as I had. But there's another answer, too, one we don't talk about as much, which is that some things get buried not for any lack of a mental space to put them but for their very unfathomableness and steadfast refusal to make sense. For me, Old Man Moss' handling of the Benton Boys had been just that, something I'd sublimated completely in the years following not because the event—the events—had been forgotten, but because I simply hadn't the means of processing them up until that night; the night I climbed the massive tower crane in downtown Seattle and came face to face with the brute. The night the string of gruesome murders that had plagued the city for months had, at last, come to an end.

"I don't see anything," said Billy the Skid, his boozy breath seeming to billow with each syllable, as he stood beside me and squinted up at the crane. "Who would it be? Construction's been halted for months, even I know that."

"I didn't say 'who,' I said 'what,' as in what is that, right there?" I pointed to where the gray figure could once again be seen (ascending not the ladder inside the scaffolding but the tower itself, like some kind of huge spider). "Do you see it? Like a man, and yet somehow not a man. And look, it's got someone thrown over its shoulder. It's right there, damn you!"

Billy only shook his head. "Whatever you say, boss." He chuckled as he made his way back to his shopping cart. "Someone thrown over his shoulder. I say if you can't handle Thunderbird you ought to leave the drinking to me. Who the hell did 'ya think it was? The Belltown Brute? Ha! And I suppose he ..."

But I wasn't listening, not really. I was still watching the gray man, the gray *thing,* ascend the tower—the hammerhead, I've heard them called—its tail swinging like a cobra (yes, yes, it had a *tail*), its ashen skin seeming to catch the lightning and throw it back, its cone-shaped head turning to face me.

Yes. Yes, it could be. Still ... was it even possible? Well, no, to be frank—it wasn't. But then, everything about the summer of '79 and what had happened to the Benton Boys and Old Man Moss' ancient Jewish magik had been impossible. That didn't change the fact that it had happened—and it *had* happened—hadn't it?

I didn't know for sure, no more than I knew whether the entry point to the crane would be locked or if I had the courage to scale the ladder or if lightning would strike as I climbed killing me just as dead as the Benton Boys. In the end I was certain of only one thing—one thing alone as I gazed up at the tower crane and watched its great jib swing in the wind. And that was that if what I suspected was true, I was at least partially responsible—for the Benton Boys, for the string of murders across Seattle and the so-called "Belltown Brute," all of it.

And that meant I had a responsibility to do something. Indeed, that I was the only person who could.

They'd had names, of course. Rusty, Jack, and Colton—otherwise known as the Benton Boys. But their individual identities had long since been subsumed by the group, the pack—I'm sure if you would have caught any single one of them alone they'd have been just as agreeable as could be. The rub, of course, was that they were never alone—that was something those who challenged them learned quickly. I learned it the day I was to meet Colton at the flagpole after school to settle our differences and he didn't show; which left Aaron and I to hoof it home feeling both victorious and relieved, at least, that is, until we rounded his block —and found them waiting for us. All three of them.

I wish I could say I was shocked that Aaron got the worst of it—it was my fight, after all, not his—but the truth of it was the Benton Boys' race-hatred was well known, and they weren't about to miss a chance to thrash a genuine Jew. Not when his idiot friend had created such a perfect opportunity. And so the racial epitaphs flew, faster even than the Boys' fists—kike, shylock, yid, Christ-killer, a few I'd never even heard before—and poor Aaron bled, and by the time it was done we'd both suffered concussions and Aaron had lost a tooth and Old Man Moss had begun screaming—in Yiddish—from his door, calling the Boys chazers and hitsigers and paskudniks, and informing them the police were already on their way. Which they weren't, actually, because Old Man Moss didn't trust anyone in a uniform.

Regardless, the Benton Boys promptly fled, and after a brief sojourn in the emergency room we were back in Aaron's front yard—just sitting there on the porch with his parents and watching the shadows lengthen across the grass. That's when I first heard his old man utter the word "golem," which he pronounced *goy-lem,* drawing a stern rebuke from Aaron's mother, who said, quickly, "Feh! And bring tsores upon us? Oy vey! *Mishegas. "*

The Old Man only snorted. "It is Mishegas to do nothing." He stroked Aaron's hair absently. "No. An eye for an eye. A tooth for an actual tooth."

"Bubbala ..."

"No. *Meesa masheena.* So it will be."

And nothing more was said—not by the Old Man or by Aaron's mother or by anyone present at all.

By the time I saw Old Man Moss again, Spring was moving rapidly toward Summer and we'd been out of school for nearly two weeks—long enough to have already tired of jumping into the river and/or bicycling out to Shelly Lake; which, in case you were wondering, were the only things to do in Benton, during that summer or any other. I was luckier than most in that I had a lawn mowing business to occupy my time—mostly for friends and family, the Mosses included— which is what I was doing when Aaron tapped me on the shoulder and asked if I could lend he and his father a quick hand.

"Is it out of this heat?" I remember shouting over the lawnmower—which was louder than most—the sweat running in rivers down my face and arms, "Because I'm dying here, and that's no joke."

"It's right here, in the garage," he said breezily, but seemed uneasy as I killed the motor and sponged my brow. "Look ... not a word about this, okay? And, please, don't laugh. Whatever you do. He—he's touchy about his art."

I think I just looked at him. It was fine by me; I'd no idea he was even an artist. "Sure, man. No problem." I must have leaned toward him. "What is it? Some kind of naked pictures?"

He blushed and stepped back. "No, man. Jesus. But it is—strange. Not a word now, okay?"

"Not a word," I promised, and gave him a salute.

It's funny—because the first thing I noticed upon stepping into the garage wasn't the fact that Old Man Moss was holding what appeared to be massive gray arm in his hands. Nor was it the fact that in the middle of the room stood an 8-foot-tall giant—a giant which appeared to have been fashioned from solid clay and resembled not so much a man but a hulking, naked ape. Nor was it even the thing's frightful visage or stoic, lifeless, outsized eyes.

No, it was the fact that the room was illuminated by candles and candelabrums—as opposed to bulbs or work lights or sun seeping through windows (all of which had been covered with what appeared to be black sheets). It was the fact that the garage didn't look like a garage. It looked—for all intents and purposes—like a temple.

"Ah, Thomas, by boy! *Vus machs da!* You are just in time."

It was on the tips of my lips to ask him what for when he handed me the arm, which was surprisingly heavy. "I'll need you and Aaron to hold this while I sculpt. Can you do that?"

The clay was tacky and moist beneath my fingers. I looked at Aaron, who looked back at me as if to say, *Just go with it. Humor him.*

"Sure, Mr. Moss. But—" I followed Aaron's lead as he positioned the arm against the mock brute's shoulder. "What on earth *is* it?"

His face beamed with pride as he worked the leaden clay. "Why, this is Yossele—but you may call him Josef. And he is what the rabbis of Chelm and Prague called a golem—a being created from inanimate matter. This one is devoted to *tzedakah,* or justice."

At last he stepped back and appeared to scrutinize his work. "And justice is precisely what he will bring—once he is finished. Once the *shem* has been placed in his mouth." He took a deep breath and exhaled, tentatively. "Okay, boys ... you can let go. Slowly."

I didn't know what justice had to do with art, but we did so—the clammy clay wanting to stick to our fingers, its moist touch seeming hesitant to break contact. "Aaron, won't you be a good *boychick* and bring me the *shem.* Easy does it, now. Don't drop it."

I watched as Aaron approached one of the workbenches and fetched an intricately-crafted gold box.

"Ah, yes. The *shem,* you see, is what gives the golem its power—thank you, son, *a sheynem dank.* It is what gives it the ability to move and become animated."

I glanced at Aaron, who only looked back at me uncertainly, as his father approached the golem and opened the box, the gold plating of which gleamed like a fire before the candelabrums. "This one consists of only one word—one of the Names of God, which is too sacred to be uttered here." He withdrew a slip of paper and placed it into the golem's mouth. "I shall only say *emet,* which means 'truth' ... and have done with it. And so it is finished. *Tetelestai. "* He turned and looked directly at me, I have no idea why. "The debt will be paid in full."

Nobody said anything for a long time, even as the birds tweeted outside and a siren wailed somewhere in the distance. We just stood there and stared at his creation.

At last I said, "So are you going to enter in the Fair, Mr. Moss, or what? How will you even move it?"

At which Old Man Moss only smiled, ruffling my hair, and said, "No—it is only for this moment. That is the nature of Art. *Tsaytvaylik.* Tomorrow it will be gone. Now run along and finish your lawn. I've involved you enough."

And the next day it *was* gone, at least according to Aaron, and both of us, I think, promptly forgot about it. At least until the first of the Benton Boys turned up dead, Sheriff Donner directing the recovery while his ashen-blue body bobbed listlessly against the Benedict A. Saltweather Dam.

It was June.

By July, the body of a second Benton Boy had been discovered—my very own buddy, Colton.

They'd found him in a stone quarry about fifteen miles from town—the Eureka Tile Company, as I recall—his limbs broken and bent back on themselves ("like some discarded Raggedy Ann," wrote the local paper) and his head completely gone—which caused a real sensation amongst the townsfolk as each attempted to solve the riddle and at least one woman reported having seen it: "Just floating down the river, like a pale, blue ball."

But it wasn't until Rusty was killed that things reached a fever pitch, with Sheriff Donner under attack for failing to solve the case and neighbor turning against neighbor in a kind of collective paranoia—for by this point no one could be trusted, not in such a small town, and the killer or killers might be anyone, even your spouse or best friend.

It was against this backdrop that I was able to break from my lawn duties—which had exploded like gangbusters over the summer—long enough to visit the Mosses: which would have been the day before Independence Day, 1979. A Tuesday, as I recall. It's funny I should remember that. Aaron's mother was working in her vegetable garden—just bent over her radishes like an emaciated old crone—when I arrived, and didn't even look up when I asked if Aaron was around. "He's in his room—done sick with the flu. Best put on a mask before you go." She added: "You'll find some in the kitchen."

I think I just looked at her—at her curved spine and thin ankles, her tied up hair which had gone gray as a golem. Then I went into the house and made my way toward Aaron's room, passing his parents' quarters—upon which had been hung a 'Do Not Disturb' sign and a Star of David—on the way. I didn't bother fetching a mask; I'm not sure why— maybe it was because I was already convinced that whatever Aaron had, I had too. Maybe it was because I was already convinced that by participating in the ritual we'd somehow brought a curse upon us—a curse upon Benton—that it had never been just 'art' and that it could never be atoned for, not by Aaron or myself or Old Man Moss or anybody. That we'd blasphemed the Name of the Lord and would now have to pay, just as Jack had paid, just as Colton had paid. Just as

Rusty had paid when they'd found him with his intestines wrapped around his throat and his eyeballs gouged out.

"Shut the door, please. Quickly," said Aaron as I stepped into his room—immediately noticing how dark it was, and that the windows had been completely blacked out (with the same sheets from the garage, I presumed). He added: "The light ... It—it's like it eats my eyes."

Christ—I *know*. But that's what he said: *Like it ate his eyes.*

I stumbled into a stool in the dark—it was right next to his bed—and sat down. Nor were the black sheets thick enough to completely choke the light, so that as I looked at him he began to manifest into something with an approximate shape: something I dare say was not entirely human—a thing thick and rounded and gray as the dead, like a huge misshapen rock, perhaps, or a mass of potter's clay, but with eyes. Then again it was dark enough so that I may only have imagined it—who's to say after forty years?

"Jesus, dude. What's happened to you? And where's your dad? I saw a 'Do Not Disturb' sign on his door. Is he—"

"Like me, only worse," choked Aaron, and then coughed—wetly, stickily. "Listen. I haven't much time. Do you remember the ritual ... and how we inserted the *shem* into the golem's mouth?"

"Of course," I said—and immediately started shaking my head. "Now wait a minute. You don't really think—"

"*Shut up, man.* Just *shut the fuck up.* This is important. The Benton Boys—what's happened to us—it's not a coincidence, okay? Dad—he created a golem ... do you understand? Not a work of art—not what Ms. Dickerson calls a metaphor. But a genuine, animate golem—right out of the folklore. Now, my mother called Rabbi Weiss when the murders started happening and told him what she suspected—that my dad had created Josef to avenge the Benton Boys' attack on us. And do you know what he said?"

"Aaron, Jesus, man—"

"He said this type of golem would go on killing, that it wouldn't stop with just the Benton Boys but would continue on to different towns and cities—for months, years, even decades. That it could make itself invisible—at least to anyone who hadn't a hand in creating it—and thus go about killing with complete efficiency; and that not even bullets could stop it, only the hand of its creator or someone who had assisted in that creation—by removing from its mouth the one thing that allowed it to move in the first place ... the Holy Shem, the slip of parchment upon which was written one of the secret Names of God."

He gripped my arm suddenly and I could tell by his cold, clammy embrace that it wouldn't be long; that his flesh had become like clay and his blood had turned thick as mud. "It's you, Thomas, don't you see? You! Only you can stop it now, only you can—"

But I didn't hear anything else he had to say, for I'd scrambled to the door and burst back into the hall. And then I ran, ran as though the world could not contain me, faster and faster and further yet—across forty years and from every type of responsibility—into drugs and alcohol and the cold numbness of the streets. Into a dream of forgetfulness which ended only when I saw the man who was not a man scaling the ghostly tower crane near our ramshackle encampment in Belltown. Until I went to the base of it, and, finding its gate lazed open, mounted the ladder at its center. And began to climb.

I was nearing the top—although still a good fifty feet away—when there was a sound, a series of sounds, actually, *thunk—thunk—thunk,* like a ham bouncing down metal stairs, and something sprinkled my face. That's when I realized that what had fallen (and bounced off the beams) was in fact a human head. By then, of course, it was gone, and I was continuing my ascent: trying not to acknowledge how the city had become so small or that lightning could strike at any instant or that the shaft of the crane was swaying woozily in the wind. Trying and mostly succeeding—at least, that is, until I reached the top, whence I climbed onto the platform next to the operator's cab (which was hanging wide open) and proceeded to vomit, although whether it was from a fear of heights or the smell of decomposition from the cab I couldn't have said.

Nor was I surprised to find that the compartment was stuffed full of bodies and body parts, like a veritable meat locker ... filled with arms and legs and heads and torsos ... or that when I turned away to retch again I saw the golem itself at the end of the crane's long jib—just crouched there in a kind of lotus position, as if he—it—were meditating. As if it—he—were waiting for me.

I can see you, Josef, I thought as the American flag crackled at the back of the crane and the great jib swung languidly in the wind ... *Can you see me?*

And then I began moving forward, slowly, tentatively—the rails of the jib like ice beneath my grip.

You can, can't you? I thought, and knew that it was so. *Tell me, Josef. Why is it you think I was spared—why I've been spared all these years— when your other creators were turned into little more than pillars of salt? Have you ever thought about that?*

Lightning flashed in the distance and turned everything white—turned the golem white—so that its monstrous features fell into stark relief; so that its cone-shaped head shown like a knife.

We are bound together, after all—don't pretend I don't know that. Even as I know you can hear me—just as plain as though I were speaking. And I ask you again—have you thought about it? Because I have.

Thunder rumbled as I drew to within twenty feet of him and paused, wondering just how I would go about it, how I would remove the *shem*. At last I said, "You were created not by God but by a man and the sages before him—now you must return to your dust. Do you understand that? It is not now, nor has it ever been—nor will it ever be—your earth to walk. It is time to go, Josef. It is long past time."

He—it—whatever—just looked at me, its slanted gray eyes inert, uninhabited—lifeless—and yet, *not.* And it occurred to me that creation was itself a kind of blasphemy; a fracturing of some perfect, unfathomable thing into something separate and purely reducible—something alone, something apart. That it was, in a sense, a cruelty. And if that were the case—wasn't it at least possible that the golem—

But then it was *moving*—suddenly, impossibly, and I was stumbling back along the gangway, and before I could do much of anything it had leapt upon me and begun gnashing its teeth—at which instant I jammed my fist into its mouth and groped for the *shem,* and whereupon finding it, yanked it free.

At that it had simply collapsed, its full weight pinning me to the gangway, and its body had broken apart like so much old masonry as its arms and legs snapped in two and its head rolled back from its shoulders—to promptly shatter against the steel mesh floor.

That's when the rains came, washing away the clay and drenching my hair and clothes, which were a beggar's clothes, until finally I rolled upon the gangway and peered down at our encampment—which was visible only because of Billy the Skid's battery-powered light—and realized, abruptly, that I still gripped the *shem.* The Holy Shem.

The Secret Name of God.

I didn't move, didn't breath, for what seemed a long time. In the end, I merely turned my fist and opened it— letting the slip of parchment fall. Watching as it fluttered into the void.

And then I slept.

At length I dreamed, of Benton and summer and freshly-cut grass ... and the first time I'd had matzo; as well as of Aaron and his parents and my parents too, whom I hadn't seen or dreamed of in years.

And when at last I awakened I did so not to the gray ceiling of my tent but a swirl of seagulls and the entire sky.

"Do it," Orley urged, and though I didn't look at him, I could feel those earnest brown eyes looking at me—eyes that always seemed just a little too intense, as if he might burst into tears or kick your ass at any moment.

"We made a pact, kid," said Kevin, his voice low, his intonation world-weary—even though he was the same age as the rest of us—Han Solo to the core, at least for today. "Besides, this was your idea."

I hesitated, the sharpened stick wavering, as the big, green caterpillar inched across the pavement. "I know." I watched as the insect's bulbous sections undulated, rising and falling, glistening in the sun. "It's just that—"

"Here," said Orley.

He took his own stick and used it to roll the caterpillar onto its back, where it curled into a fetal position and promptly froze, looking like a shrimp at the Chuck Wagon buffet, its multitude of little legs ceasing to move, its tiny antennae holding perfectly still.

"Okay, read that passage. The one about daring to approach the gods. You know, where it talks about blood and danger and becoming like gods ourselves. I saw you bookmark it."

I looked at the book, *The Encyclopedia of Death and Dying*—which was lying atop my orange nylon schoolbag precisely where I'd left it—and stood, hefting the volume and cutting to the mark. The sun passed behind a cloud as I read, "Participants in blood sacrifice rituals often experience a sense of awe, danger, or exaltation, because they are daring to approach the gods who create, sustain, and destroy life. Therefore, morale is strengthened by the ritual killing, because the group has itself performed the godlike act of destruction—and is now capable of renewing its own existence."

There was a slight breeze, which seemed to give the proceedings a funereal air, and I continued, "The underlying philosophical assumption is that life must pass through death."

Orley said, "That's it. Okay. So." He looked from me to Kevin—earnestly, intensely—gripping the sharpened stick. "Considering what's ahead of us ..." He paused, letting that sink in. "I think we all know what we have to do." He added: "And why."

We thought about it, the sun beating down, the breeze jostling our hair. The lake. The sword. The visitations in our dreams. We knew.

"So I say we get to it ... before the Valley Boys show up and it's too late. *Way* too late."

I looked at Kevin—who just looked at me with that Zen Master expression of his but seemed to confirm—before again crouching by the caterpillar. And then we all gripped our sticks—and prepared to do something really shitty.

By the time the sun re-emerged the caterpillar had crawled across the sidewalk and into the grass—leaving us more than a little red-faced, not to mention uncertain as to what had just happened. Mostly, I think, we were just relieved.

"I couldn't do it," said Kevin wistfully, "Not with the kid here."

I raised my eyebrows and looked at him, as if to say: Fucking *what,* dude?

He started to smile but caught it.

Orley elbowed me. "Hey, hey, why didn't you?" He looked at me earnestly, calmly—as though he were all ears, all understanding. Then he deadpanned, "It was the gay thing, wasn't it?"

And then they both laughed, falling about on the grass, even as I ignored them, thinking about it.

"I don't know. It just ... it felt like ..." I looked at them in the sun. "Like we would be killing ourselves ... not the caterpillar. Or a part of ourselves. Like, a version of ourselves. The ideal version."

They paused, looking at each other, processing this.

"So the gay thing," said Orley, and held up his hand—which Kevin promptly high-fived.

I must have just stared at them as they bumped fists and swiped palms. "What's that? Foreplay?"

And then they were both crawling toward me, sneering menacingly, and by the time the Valley Boys rumbled up in their chopped and channeled Chevy (as opposed to our learning permits and BMX bikes), everything had devolved into an out-of-control wrestling match; a match which ended only when Todd Benson, the leader of our bullies, shouted, "Are you faggots finished? Because there's a lot of miles between here and the lake. And it's getting late."

"Jesus," he said as we clambered into the backseat, the gear in our schoolbags clanking and thumping. "You think you brought enough?"

"Should have charged them by weight," added Mickelson. He twisted in the front passenger seat and glared at us. "You runts planning on camping there or moving in?"

Just Mickelson. This was going to be easier than we thought.

"Listen," snapped Orley. "Hearing you run your mouth wasn't part of the—"

"Money," said Benson, and reached over his shoulder. "Twenty now, twenty when we get there. As agreed."

We all looked at each other.

At last we dug into our jeans and pulled out our bills—Orley and I, at any rate (I had a five left over from my allowance and he had some ones, tips from his job at the golf course). Kevin, meanwhile, had reached into his backpack and was fishing around for something, straining. It couldn't have been easy; he hadn't taken it off. None of us had.

A moment later he withdrew a purple Crown Royal bag and handed it to Mickelson, whose hand dropped from the weight of it. "Is this a fucking joke?"

"Nope. Seven dollars, counted and rolled."

Mickelson just stared at him—as though he might jab him right then and there.

"Take it, asshole," said Benson. He glanced at Kevin through the rear-view mirror. "It's the money he's been saving for *Star Wars* figures."

Mickelson took the bag and appeared to set it on the floor before turning up the stereo and cocking his arm out the window, still shaking his head. Moments later, looking in the side-view mirror, he said, "There they are. Right on time."

We all glanced at each other—before craning to look through the rear window and seeing Jud Spelvin's rodded out Ford Falcon bearing down upon us, its chromed stacks glinting and its headlights shining, and its cab virtually crammed with pasty-faced seniors, at least one of whom I recognized as Buddy LaCombe—the *third* biggest asshole at

Prosperous High. And, considering twenty was all we'd had and we planned to hit and run, this was a problem.

I looked at Benson through the rearview mirror and saw him smirk at our reaction.

"Awww," he said, and pretended to pout. "Why so sad? You didn't think it would just be us, did you?"

But nobody said anything, just stared straight ahead at the road, the road that would take us to Mirage Lake and the thing we'd left buried under the brush, as Bob Seger and the Silver Bullet Band sang *Fire Lake* and the sun crept toward the stark, blue horizon, and shafts of light pierced the trees— *like spears through a sacrifice,* I thought. Or sunlight through a cathedral.

It's still hard to believe, what happened next. But then, it's *all* hard to believe, especially now, almost 40 years later. Suffice it to say that we were only minutes from the lake when the deer ran out in front of us and caused Benson to hit the brakes— throwing us against the bucket seats (and Orley, who was in the middle, halfway into the forward cab) even as Spelvin's Falcon rammed us from behind, knocking us right back. To this day I wonder if she—*it,* our Lady of the Lake, our Thing from Another World—had something to do with it. If she had reached out from her watery tomb and *guided* the animal into our path—to ensure its intended servants reached their destination. To guarantee its release after so many years trapped beneath the lake.

Regardless, they were all gathered around the bumpers when we made our escape, clambering out the driver's side door (which had been left ajar) and scurrying into the trees— our packs and gear jangling, our shoes scraping the gravel—so that Benson at least became aware of our movement and quickly alerted the rest. This touched off a footrace which wound from the side of the road all the way to Beggar's Dead-fall, which we climbed as they went around—before reversing course and backtracking through the brush, eventually stumbling upon the very same trail we'd taken last time. This we followed (after standing for a period with our hands on our knees and laughing, catching our breath) to the far side of the lake.

Where a massive, overgrown, arrowhead-shaped thing, a blue-black thing, an ancient and broken thing—a thing perhaps only we could see—lay half-buried amongst the trees.

We'd been staring at it for maybe five minutes when Kevin wandered away from us and paused at the water, where he shielded his eyes from the sunset and mumbled, "They're back. The hands, the twelve-string guitar ..."

I followed his gaze, shielding my eyes also, to where the black sword could again be seen in the middle of the lake. As before, it was held aloft by a pair of slim, beautiful hands. "Wrong again—kid. I told you: It's Stormbringer, sister to Mournblade, runesword of Elric, the last emperor of Melniboné."

"No," said Orley, approaching us, "It's neither of those." He shouldered between us and stood with his hands on his hips, like a superhero. "It's Excalibur, obviously. Held aloft by the Lady of the Lake, waiting to be claimed."

The truth of it was, it was all those things and none of those things, but we didn't know that yet, didn't know much of anything—we were only 15. But we knew it was real, whatever it was, and that something associated with it had been visiting us in our dreams. We also knew each other, and so understood that each of us was seeing something totally unique to ourselves: Kevin was learning guitar, his AWOL father's twelve-string, and thus naturally saw an instrument. I was obsessed with the works of Michael Moorcock—Elric, in particular—and had been trying to write something similar. And Orley had been reading about Camelot (and struggling with Middle English) ever since his mother had brought home a copy of *Le Morte d'Arthur* from the Salvation Army. More than any of that, though, we knew what we had to do— although we still didn't know why or how—and it was to that end that we set about our work, breaking off spear-length branches from the nearby trees and whittling them as sharp as we could, fashioning still others into makeshift rowing paddles, and each taking turns blowing up the raft by working the little handpump we'd stolen from White Elephant.

By the time we were ready, the sky was completely red, like Mars, or Vulcan, and we were beginning to feel the press of time—perhaps the surest indication that one has moved closer to adulthood than childhood. But then we were adrift, and all such concerns were forgotten, and though we struggled at first to coordinate our paddles, it became evident soon enough that we would reach the swords, the guitar, *the anomaly,* well before dark—and so steeled ourselves as best we could; mostly by talking about our dreams, both those experienced by night and those conceived of by day—for they were pertinent, all of them, to what lie ahead.

"She showed me a vision in which I was being awarded the Medal of Honor," said Orley at last, working his paddle, staring straight ahead. "Carter himself was the one who affixed it around my neck."

The little raft rocked, dark water slapping, but nobody expressed doubt.

"I was a best-selling author," I said, quietly, solemnly. "Like Stephen King. But really, really good-looking."

"I was a rock star," said Kevin. "Bigger even than Elvis."

We rowed, drawing closer to the thing.

"It is the future you see," said Kevin in his best Yoda voice.

Nobody laughed.

"Maybe," said Orley. "That is, if we free her from the lake. If we—I don't know—return her to her ship or something. Leastwise that's how I interpreted it."

"Me too," I said.

Kevin leaned forward, rocking the boat. "But why the swords and the guitar? And why can't she leave the lake? What the hell *is* she, even?"

We all thought about that as a loon cried somewhere across the water.

"Maybe she's too weak," I said. "Maybe her body is ... mutilated or something—from the crash." I looked to where the black sword seemed to hover just above the surface of the water—as sinister as it was eldritch, precisely as I'd always imagined it. And below that, her—the woman in the water's—hand; her thin, beautiful hand, deaden-blue from the depths.

"Maybe that's just how she establishes contact," I said. "How she gets your attention, and holds it. I honestly wouldn't be surprised if all that just goes away—like a mirage—when we get there."

"Nah. Then why—"

But then, as if to confirm, the hand *did* begin to go away, to lower, taking the sword with it—as if, indeed, it *had* been just a prop, just bait to get us closer.

"Fuck!" shouted Orley. He jerked his paddle, doubling his efforts. "Hurry up! Row!"

But it was too late; it was gone. The sword, the deaden-blue hand, all of it.

I'm not sure how long we floated there, just looking at each other. All I know is that by the time we busted out the flashlights the color had bled from the hills and the temperature had dropped significantly; enough so that our decision not to bring coats (there was only so much room in our backpacks, after all) seemed foolhardy and brash.

Regardless, it was Kevin who first saw something, jolting as we trained our lights into the murky water and blurting, in a voice that was one part excitement and at least two parts terror, "Holy shit! I saw her! I saw her! She swam right beneath the raft!"

I remember Orley just freezing and staring at me—earnestly, intensely—before we both dropped to our bellies and shoved our flashlights against the water, angling the beams as far beneath the raft as we could while each taking a side—the hope being that we wouldn't upend the entire boat. Kevin meanwhile actually reached into the drink and felt around, which seemed unwise to me at the time and more than a little out of character, reckless, even. Crazy-brave.

That's when it happened. That's when the girl, but really the xenoform, the multi-dimensional being, the *thing*, just floated up: her face emerging like some porcelain doll and her blue-black hair swirling (like tentacles, I thought, or the snakes in Medusa's hair), her drowned, all-white eyes staring. That's also when she reached up with arms as thin as paper dowels—famine arms, Buchenwald arms—and pulled me into the lake.

What happened next happened very fast—or so I've been told, because it sure didn't seem fast at the time. Indeed, it felt like the longest dozen seconds of my life. All I know is that the girl-thing sank rapidly, briefly, dragging me along with her, before just as suddenly releasing me—discarding me, as it were—and disappearing.

Except she *didn't* disappear, not really, which I found out as soon as I burst back to the surface. Rather, she had leapt from the water and tried to beach herself on the raft—but had overshot it—so that she now hung off its opposite side: flopping and struggling, fighting and twisting, like a fish out of water, or an animal against its leash.

For she was connected, you see, to a kind of umbilical cord, which began at her back, stretched taught across the boat, and vanished into the cold, dark water. Nor was the cord at rest but seemed to be contracting like a great rubber band—pulling her back toward the surface, exerting what must have been a great force. That's when it hit me that I *knew* what the cord was, and that it was neither inorganic material nor biological tissue—if anything, it was both—just as I knew that she had not so much attacked me as merely glommed onto me in desperation.

Because something had happened while we touched beneath the water, something like telepathy, or accelerated osmosis. And I understood suddenly why she had been unable to escape; and why, too, she had called out to us, beckoned us, and suggested we do things like sharpen sticks. More importantly, I understood what she, *it,* was capable of; that the futures she had shown us were not only possible but easily within reach—*if* we but freed her and reunited her with her ship (which was so much more than a ship!). If we but stayed true to our purpose and did our allotted part. And I knew beyond any doubt what I—*we*—had to do.

"Don't let her slip back into the water!" I cried suddenly, kicking toward the raft, grabbing one of the hand-holds. "Keep her inside the boat!"

But the pull of the life-line—for that's what it was and that's what it was tethered to: a *life-pod,* something which had ejected from the ship upon crashing and sunk to the bottom of the lake—was too strong, too resistant, and she began to slip backward across the boat.

That's when Orley stood upon his knees in the raft and brought his makeshift spear down as hard as he could, stabbing the cord precisely at its center—causing blue-black ichor to geyser like blood. Kevin quickly joined him, and I after that, so that the cord was weakened even as the girl-thing struggled and screamed—to the point that she was able to free herself at last and slide back into the water, looking, in the instants before she vanished, not like a girl at all, but a gelatinous mass. A thing without limbs or extremities. A kind of blue-black worm.

Needless to say, the raft did not survive the encounter. And yet we were able to paddle at least partly to shore before it deflated completely— enough so that the remaining distance was easily traversed, primarily by floating on our backs while kicking.

And then we were huddled in the tent like sardines, the fire having been left to die and our over-clothes hung from the branches to dry— nobody making gay jokes, nobody saying anything—as our minds raced and dwelt on the future, as our sharpened sticks stood sentinel, canted in the sand.

I wish I could say that when Benson and his gang showed up we drew on some previously unknown strength and kicked their Rich Kid asses; that we chased them all the way back to their fancy cars and tucked and rolled seats and kicked in their doors and fenders; although we really would do that later, not to them personally but to guys like them, in those dog days immediately after high school— when Orley had yet to join the Army and I'd yet to lose my mother, and L.A. was just a twinkle in Kevin's eye.

Instead they caught us completely by surprise, knocking the tent over and rolling us up in it—like a giant snowball—after which they proceeded to kick and punch us mercilessly—before dragging us out by our feet and gloating over us in the sun: *Like trolls,* I remember thinking. Or Tolkien's fucking orcs.

"Well now look at this," said Benson, and paused to hawk up phlegm. "If it isn't our little faggots—just cozied up like lemmings." He pursed his lips and spat, causing green slime to splatter my cheek. "Our thievin' little douche-flutes, just letting their freak flags fly."

"And sitting on the rest of our gas money," said Mickelson. "I can guarantee it."

"Oh?" Benson raised his brow, as if he hadn't thought of that. "You're kind of the leader, Orley. Is that true?"

Orley just looked at him, his mouth bleeding, his cheek scuffed and bruised. At last he said, "We used it to pay your mother. She said that's what triple-penetration costs."

A couple of them laughed—Mickelson and Spelvin, I think—and Benson shot them a look. At length he said, "Funny—as always." He paused, cocking his head. "You look thirsty. Buckey. Give me your cup."

He held out his hand without looking and Buckey placed in it a large container, one of those 32-ounce super tankards you get at Zip Trip or 7-11, minus its lid. "The stink bugs are terrible this year, as I'm sure you've noticed. Buckey here left this out in the sun too long," He smelled the cup's contents, wrinkling his nose—then motioned to Spelvin and Mickelson, who snatched Orley up by his arms and held him, even as two others grappled his head and began prying

54

his mouth open. "These will probably tickle a little as they go down. A lot of them are still alive ..."

Then he tipped the cup and its contents poured out onto Orley's face, into his mouth—the soda spattering his cheeks, the little bugs scrambling helter-skelter over his lips—before he chocked once, suddenly, violently, and began *chewing,* jerking his head free of their hands, smiling like a lunatic.

"Protein!" he exclaimed, and spit something out, a shell, maybe, or a leg. "Thank you, sir! May I have another!"

And then there was a commotion which sent a ripple through their ranks and caused them to stand apart—staring toward the lake, into the sun, where a lone figure stood slight as a wraith, its hair sopping wet, clinging to its face, its skinny arms held straight at its sides.

"Who's that? Is that your mother?" —Spelvin, I think, attempting to sound cocksure but really only sounding frightened and small.

I looked to where the girl-thing stood nude and alone, her hair entwined with seaweed, her one visible eye white as milk. None of us said anything as the Benson Gang approached her and slowly gathered around—triangulating her, isolating her.

"Well, well," said Benson, "This makes sense." He turned to face us, regarding us slyly. "So this is what brought you pervs all the way out here. And here I thought you were just queer."

He looked at the girl again, who couldn't have been more than 15, same as us, and said, mockingly, "Is that seaweed in your hair, or are you just more experienced than you look?" Everyone tittered; a few of them groaned.

"Careful," said Mickelson, "Or she'll sic her boyfriends on us." He shouted over his shoulder: "Isn't that right, douche-flutes?"

But none of us said anything, just continued to stare at the girl, whose milky eye regarded Benson plainly, flatly, as though here were a lifeform hardly worth shooing away; a tsetse fly, maybe, or a gnat.

"You know, it might just be me," said Benson, and moved closer, "but I get the impression she doesn't want to be friends."

He started walking around her slowly, checking her out, looking her up and down. "That how it's going to be, sis? You going to just give us the cold, blue shoulder?"

"Meh, ease off her, Todd," someone said—Jud Hartman, a sometimes decent guy whom I hadn't even realized was with them. "She's obviously suffered some sort of trauma. Probably thought she was drowning, or something."

"Drowning, or something," said Benson, and stepped close to her ear. "What do you say, sis? Were you drowning—or something? Is that why you're just as naked as a jaybird? Or are you just some coked-out whore, turning tricks in the sticks?" He grabbed her by the shoulder suddenly. "Face me when I'm talking to ..."

And then his hand was burning—burning and crisping away—and he was stumbling back over the sand, screaming, hyperventilating, the blood and bones of his arm gleaming, before the sun dipped behind a cloud and all hell broke loose. Before it became clear to us, so very, very clear, that the time for talking was over.

To say that what happened next was, for all intents, impossible to describe, would be to short you, Reader, in a way I am not prepared to do. More so, it would be to skip or gloss over the most salient aspect of what occurred that day; the day in which we learned just how strange and inexplicable the universe really was, and, more importantly, just how dangerous it had become—not just for us but for everything we had ever known, ever would know.

Suffice it to say that when the lightning-like bolts erupted from the girl-thing's eyes, they instantly connected with (and paralyzed) virtually everyone present—Kevin, Orley and myself included. And here is where it gets so strange—and difficult to describe—for what happened next was like, a kind of mass hallucination, one in which all of us, I think, felt we could read the thing's thoughts; not only that, but that we could see where it was from.

And where it was from was hideous beyond measure: a place as barren and blue and seemingly lifeless as the girl's body itself—a place, a planet, a dimension, where everything that had ever lived had long since been devoured and consumed, and where the husks of those drained of their lifeforce had, at last, formed piles as high as mountains.

It was, in short, a kind of Hell, and what we learned in those moments—the moments we stood paralyzed and alone, trapped, each of us, by the lightning-like force—was that this was the fate of all the worlds they, her species, had encountered (via scouts, just as she); and that this was simply what they *did:* They *fed,* and more, that they had learned to create entirely new dimensions, entirely new timelines, exactly toward that end—all to satisfy their ever-growing need.

And we learned one thing more: which was that although Earth was next—*our* Earth, the Earth of this particular dimension, this timeline—a thousand more might yet be created, and that one of these would be the Earth upon which Orley would walk as a war hero and I a bestselling author, and where Kevin would be a rock star, bigger even than Elvis. A place where we wouldn't be losers at all but gods, receiving a blowjob from all the world. The place she had promised us in our dreams—and which would now come. Whether we liked it or not.

For, having chosen us for our very softness and empathy, and loving us—insofar as she was able to do so—for rescuing her, she intended to keep her promise.

One thing is certain, and that is that everyone who was standing when she let loose the bolts was no longer standing when they disappeared—including, to our surprise, the girl-thing herself, who collapsed even as we collapsed, as the Benson Gang collapsed, their bodies shriveled like prunes and their faces sucked in, as though they'd simply imploded when their life-force had been extracted, which, I suppose, they *had.*

Then it was over and we had climbed to our feet, shaking ourselves off, grateful to be alive, but aghast at the destruction and loss of life all around us. For the Benson Gang was dead, each and every one, and their nude bodies had become husks— their clothes having burned away in the incident, I supposed—which rattled in the sand as they were buffeted by the breeze and eventually just dis-incorporated, blowing away like dandelion seeds.

As for the thing, we knew *exactly* what had happened (we'd been in her head, after all, at least that's how we interpreted it, just a few moments before): she'd expended all her energy in the extraction of their life-force and yet wouldn't gain from the transfer until it had been converted by her system, a process which might take hours, even days.

Unless, we knew, we could get her to her ship, which had begun to glow amidst the trees like a white-hot iron and which would restore her to full health if she were just able to join with it—an outcome which seemed increasingly unlikely as we watched her try to stand and come crashing back down, her arms barely capable of breaking her fall and her legs all but useless in their compromised condition. So, too, did we know that any attempt to touch her would result in the same type of injury suffered by Benson. And thus we could only watch as she began to crawl toward her ship across the rocks and sand, pleased that she seemed to be gaining strength with each foot traveled—but knowing, also, that it would not be enough.

"Jesus, look at her face," said Orley at last, and when I followed his gaze I saw that her features had begun to droop and her hair to fall out, so that she was starting to look like Jason Voorhees in *Friday the 13th*(when he bursts from the water at the end of the movie), her brow sagging and her mouth twisting, her head balding, her eyes mismatched.

"She's using all her strength to get to her ship," I said, "and can no longer maintain the ruse. But I don't she's going to make it."

"And yet she might," said Kevin, his freckles standing out harsh and clear in the sun and his red hair a veritable fire. "She might."

At length Orley said, "I feel sorry for them if she does."

I think I just looked at him: at his earnest, intense eyes and his unruly mop of hair, at his shitty, threadbare clothes because his mother was too poor to dress him. "What do you mean?" I said.

"I mean everything—*everyone.* All our parents, all our siblings. Everything we have ever known, just *gone.* Like Benson and his friends."

We watched as she tried to stand, surer-footed this time, stronger, but then came crashing back down.

"That's not it," I said. "You were there. Other timelines will be created, other dimensions, all of them like this one. All of them populated by the same people. It's just that one of them will—"

"Be modified and left alone, I know. But what about the others? What of the millions, the trillions, whatever, that will exist only to be killed, to be harvested, like cattle? What about this world, right here?"

I looked to where the thing was again crawling to its feet—it was no longer proper to call it a she—its fingers and toes shrinking as I watched.

"But they're all the same, don't you see? They're all the same thing, just replicated a thousand-fold. How can ..." I paused, staring at him.

"Are they?" he said.

I continued looking at him, the sun beating upon our heads, the breeze jostling our hair. When I glanced at Kevin I found him already looking at me.

"She's going to make it," he said—calmly, meditatively. "Look."

We peered beyond him and saw that it was so, that the thing was up again and stumbling toward the trees. Stumbling, not crawling, as the arrowhead-shaped ship glowed and the brush we'd piled atop it caught fire, *poofing* like bags full of air opened too quickly, smoking like fireworks about to explode.

"Jesus," I mumbled. "Do you think we're evolved enough to ..."

I glanced at our sticks only several feet away, canted in the sand, their shafts crude but straight— then at the thing, which was nearly to its ship. And the truth of it is I was running before I'd even made a conscious decision to do so, running with the friends I'd had since 4th grade at Broadway Elementary, both of whom beat me to the pikes. Nor did we stop to think about it as we chased the thing down like chieftains and Orley delivered the first blow, lancing its back decisively and pinning it to the earth as I slid mine into what would have been its ribcage and Kevin impaled its neck, all of which caused the thing to struggle furiously even as it tried to scream—this most assuredly—but found it had no mouth; as it melted away from our sticks like butter and reconstituted itself on the go, finally closing to within a few feet of its ship before Orley ran it through its back yet again and smashed it to the ground, stopping it in its tracks—even as Kevin and I stabbed it repeatedly—the sun filtering through the pines as it shuddered and bled, its ship beginning to falter, growing cool amidst the shadows.

And yet we kept stabbing as though infected with blood-lust: exhilarated by each blow, hot for the kill, while nonetheless feeling as though we had lost something with each strike. Something of who we were and might have become. Something which felt good and bad at the same time. Like romantic love, I suppose, which we had yet to experience. Or the bite of cigarette smoke into the esophagus and lungs.

Until at last the ship lie dormant and the Thing from Another World was dead, if it had ever lived at all, at least in the way we understood it. And then we just stood there for a time amongst the shafts of light and brooded in our youth and vigor and passion; there in July of 1980 in the sweltering heat and humidity of the day. There in the forest by the lake, which was shot through with orange and gold, in the brief, burning cathedral of summer.

I'm not sure how long it took us to get home, although we were able to scramble aboard a freight train at Hunter's Rock—we could tell it was bound for Spokane—which cut the overall time considerably. All I remember is that I became fascinated by my friend's faces as we sat between cars and watched the land pass, the late-afternoon sun painting everything redden-gold as the tracks clacked and livestock raised their heads, as we let our minds wander and tried not to think too hard about what had happened, nor our role in it.

Orley for his part was trying to sleep, and though we at first made sport of preventing him from doing so, we eventually relented and let him be. He had a job, after all, unlike either of us. Still, I watched him as the train rocked and he dozed, knowing even then that nothing would ever come easy for him; that he'd been born into the kind of poverty that either perpetuated itself or was overcome by sheer grit and determination. I never told him, later, how much I'd admired his bravery and humor during the whole ordeal, nor how often I'd looked to him as something I might one day like to be: just a skinny guy, perhaps, but one with an indomitable spirit and a spit-in-your-eye confidence; a person as earnest as he was intense and who rose to the occasion and did what had to be done, not to mention one who possessed an incredible head of hair, like one of the Beatles, I remember thinking, or Derick Wildstar.

Kevin meanwhile was watching the landscape pass, his demeanor just as mellow and Zen as could be, as though we hadn't faced the end of the world at all but just enjoyed the great outdoors and built a campfire to bullshit around. Kevin was and remains one of the biggest weavers of bullshit I have ever known—not the least of which is his bullshit about not being very bright—and yet there was a truth to him as he looked out over the fields that could not be denied, for he was also grounded in a way I have never seen, just centered like a rock, accepting life as it was and hacking whatever it dealt him. And what it had dealt him so far was a broken home and poverty not much less than Orley's. And, also not less than Orley, an epic head of hair.

I had to smile a little while looking at that hair: Donny Bonaduce? Why not. With hair like that, Donny could never be far. But Slim Pickens, too. Someone with a big heart and even bigger generosity. And I knew even then what kind of friend he'd be as an adult, which was the kind you could couch-surf with when your wife kicked you out even if you hadn't seen him in thirty years. That friend. The kind that embodied the very word.

I guess it goes without saying that we never became gods or got a blowjob from the entire world, but then, who does, really? At the end of the day you're lucky if you can just make a few friends. Kevin never became a rock star and Orley never received the Medal of Honor, and I never became a best-selling author, though I've published a few books on Amazon and even took my girlfriend to dinner once on the proceeds, and that included the tip.

But we did save the world once, a long, long time ago. And it was not without cost or sacrifice.

And that should count for something. Even if it is, like us, like you, just one of so many things that might have been.

We're at our breaking point, myself and Taylor—even the Captain sounds hang-dogged and defeated. "Just a little further," he keeps saying into his mic, as if repeating the lie will somehow make it true, "We're almost there. Feel that moisture in the air? That's the Acidalia Canal and the next Oasis. Just stay sharp. Oh, and Taylor? Quit blowing debris into the fucking pools. Nothing pisses a settler off worse than arriving to a dirty pool."

I laugh aloud at that, knowing Taylor is doing the same. *As if.* We haven't seen a transport or a settler in weeks. Has immigration to the Formerly Red Planet slowed? We don't know.

I look at the houses, so pristine and white, so uniform, their black windows glinting, resolving to ask the next settler I see (and to hell with the no-contact edict). But then something rustles amidst the stalks (so, too, is there a vibration in the air) and I move: having learned, since my arrival at Utopia Planitia, to never linger long in uncut grass; nor to dwell on what happened to the trimmers before me.

"And there she is," comes the Captain again, "As promised. One Oasis with medical rocket, right next to the Acidalia Canal. What do you have to say now, Decker? Something cute, I imagine. Go right ahead."

But the truth is, because of the whir of my light-trimmer's blades, I am not even sure if I've heard him correctly, and so ask him to repeat it, which he does. Then I pause, looking over my shoulder at Taylor (who has caught up to me in spite of his exhaustion), and we just stand there, he with his blower and I with my trimmer, until he shakes his head, slowly, and I key my headset: "So is it the end of the sector, or what? Do you see a bridge?"

His answer is garbled, indecipherable—a favorite trick of the Captain's when he doesn't want to speak. At length we hear: " ...responsible for your asses. I'm going to go in and check for—" And we lose him in a hail of static.

I look at Taylor, our eyes locked, our faces bathed in sweat. "Checking for gnomes, he says. Well? What do you think? Is he telling the truth?"

He looks at me for what seems a long time. "All I know is ... I'm done. I'm just ... done with all this. I'm sorry."

It takes me a minute to process what he's saying. "Jesus, Taylor. You don't mean—"

"Done—if there's a bridge," he says, finally, even as it becomes clear to me he has already thought this out, already looked at it from every angle, committed to it completely. "Total forfeit of bonus, I know. But—I'm taking that medical rocket. I'm going home."

At last I say, "You won't have enough money to migrate, you know that. And they'll never hire you again once you forfeit—you know that too?"

He shakes his head slowly. "It doesn't matter. Besides, I wouldn't be so sure. They've created a monster here—and they know it." He scans the green horizon—balefully, it seems. "It's never going to stop, you know. It's just going to keep growing, faster and faster, until ..."

I slap him a little, wondering if he's succumbing to the Daze. "Until what? Until what, Taylor?"

"Until they'll even hire back a forfeiter," he says, appearing to come out of it, and laughs.

I clasp his shoulder, give it a hearty shake. *"There won't be a bridge.* After twenty sectors? No way. They're greedy—not stupid." I look to the houses still ahead of us and at the overgrown grass; at the flowerbeds chocked with red-weed and the walkways overrun with Bryum moss. "Either way, we've still got this sector to clear. Unless, of course, you want to forfeit everything?"

"No way, man," he says, and seems to buck up.

And then we are moving, frustrating whatever gnomes have been moving in on us and triggering our nuclear-powered tools, our lips longing for water, our bellies grumbling, our hearts longing— knowing, praying, the Oasis is near.

I cannot decide what is the more horrific sight: the steel bridge leading to the next (and 21st) sector—or Taylor's face as he looks at it, which appears pale as the dead even though it has been deeply darkened by the sun. Worse, the Captain has yet to exit the rocket—which suggests he may have found something (i.e., the kind of trouble only gnomes can bring). So, too, is his bright red Big Trak still running (as if he saw something and had to leap off it quickly). At this point only one thing is certain—none of it bodes well for Taylor's intended departure.

When at last the Captain emerges he is holding an apple in one hand and his knife in the other, shaking his head. "Yuh, it's what I thought. They got the console. Startled 'em real good, but, well, the damage was done." He smiles cockeyed, polishing the apple on his shirt, then plops down in the hatchway and begins cutting the fruit. "It's not all bad, though. I saved the provisions."

I look at Taylor, who also appears skeptical. "They ruined the console but left the provisions? Why would they do that?" he asks.

"Like I said, I scared them off. As for the console, you know they like to strip the wires and use the copper," He bends down suddenly and picks up one of their tiny spears, touches it near the tip. "See that? It's remarkable, really. Holds the Folsom point just as snug as a virgin. What the hell are you getting at, anyway?"

"It just seems weird that—"

"What he's 'getting at' is that he's tired," I say, "And that we got at least one more sector to clear before we can get out of here. So let's bivouac and get going, before they discover our *real* ticket home—the rocket at the end of the quadrant. Yeah?"

Cap just shrugs, eating his apple. "You'll get no argument from me." But something is troubling him, because he keeps eyeing Taylor suspiciously as he cuts the fruit into wedges, looking the man up and down, taking the measure of him. After a while he says, "What I can't figure is, why all this concern over a medical rocket?"

"Forget it," I say. "Let's just eat."

"'Forget it,' he says. 'Let's just eat' ... No, no, I think we should talk about it. See, if someone goes home—that'll break up the crew. And that's something I need to know about." He pauses, the knife glinting in his hand. "How about it, Taylor? You sick? Thinking about going home?"

I glance at my friend—whose face has become red as Cap's apple from heat and frustration.

"If I was, I wouldn't need your perm—"

"Look, forget it," I say, even as the Captain stands, slowly—dropping the apple—so that we are suddenly nose to nose. I add: "No one's breaking up the crew. You'll get your bonus, don't worry. We all will."

"Not if this crew fragments, I won't," he says, coldly, flatly—still holding the knife. "That's the difference between you and me. The difference between all of us. Unless, of course, you think you'd be better—"

"Just forget it," I say, stepping back, standing down. "No one's questioning your authority. And no one's going anywhere. Isn't that right, Taylor?"

"Hmph," says Taylor. "I'm not going to be told whether I'm sick or not by no *white* company's white man—"

"—isn't that right, Taylor? We got work to do."

At length he relents. "Yeah, sure, that's right." He steps up to the hatch, which is being blocked by the Cap—then shrugs, splaying his hands. "Y'mind? Nigger's got to eat."

At last the Captain steps aside, mumbling, "Forget it. Sure, why not. Another whole sector. Fine. Take five. Take twenty. Whatever. I'm going to get started on the other side."

And then he's gone, firing up the Big Trak and rattling away, as we just look at each other, wondering if he's getting the Daze, and wondering, too, just how the hell we're going to make it—how we're going to clear another entire sector—as the sun beats down and we head into the afternoon. As the white houses look on, their dark windows glinting, and the temperatures climb, soon to be soaring, and the freshly cut grass begins to regrow at our feet.

I am pilfering a drink from the hose of one of the settlers' homes (something we are expressly forbidden to do) when the yellowjacket attacks: its legs dangling insidiously and its wings vibrating dizzyingly so that I find myself snatching up my trimmer in a panic and swinging it like a bludgeon (instead of just turning it on rationally and targeting the wasp carefully); the result being that while the fist-sized insect is vanquished a nearby window is shattered—which of course brings Taylor running (though fortunately not the Captain).

"Jesus, man! What are you—"

"Whoa, whoa, whoa, watch it," I say, quickly. "There's a wasp on the ground—somewhere. There, by the spigot."

A moment later he pauses to examine it, notably breathless from the run. "Holy shit—look at that." He prods it with the end of his blower, making sure its dead. "Bastard's are getting bigger, you notice that? Ever since they sprayed the M-4."

He stands, shaking his head, still catching his breath. "It's like I said, they've created a monster here. I'm starting to wonder if I even *want* to migrate, to tell the truth. Earth might be wasted but at least there's no bees the size of ..." He trails off, looking at the window. "Well, shit," he says, and scratches his head. "That's bad. Now what?"

I look at it too, thinking, *There's no bees on Earth at all. That's the problem.* "I don't know," I say, exhaling, "but something tells me I just spent my bonus—all of it."

"Jesus, you smell that?"

"Yeah—like rotting grass. Only ..." I look around, not recalling seeing any piles of clippings or other yard debris. "I don't see anything. There's nothing here that would account for it. What are you doing?"

"Following my nose," he says, leaning into the window, sniffing inside the house. "It's coming from in here; from—" He falls silent abruptly, his whole body freezing, tensing up. "Holy Mother of ..."

"What is it? What do you see?"

But he is no longer at the window, having instead placed his hands on his knees and begun vomiting into the bushes, his entire body heaving, trembling like an epileptic, and his blower falling to the ground, where it lolls onto its side and continues to sputter and hum.

We have tied our bandannas over our mouths and begun to explore the house, which has been overrun with crabgrass and vines of Creeping Charlie; with Canada Thistle and Purslane, with sprouts of Shepard's Purse, even as flies the size of silver dollars buzz about the body and the Captain tries to raise us—fruitlessly, of course. For it is his turn to dine on static.

But it is the body that compels me and causes me to keep returning to it (having checked the kitchen and dining area, as well as what appears to be a meditation chamber, and found nothing), batting away the flies, scattering them like dandelion seeds. It's funny, because if it weren't for the red-weed growing from its mouth and the mushroom stools in its eyes and nostrils, not to mention its green flesh, I would simply take it to be a settler who had fallen asleep on his couch—a victim, perhaps (based on his tranquil expression at death) of what we call the Daze.

As it is, I am forced only to accept it as a great mystery, one not apt to be solved by a pair of grass grunts poking around in the dark—whether we find more like it or not—at least that's what I'm thinking as I look out the gigantic window at the deck and see the large white telescope angled on its tripod. As I ignore my radio and hear Taylor shouting somewhere above, somewhere on the second landing, saying, "We got four more up here, brother from another mother! And they're all D.O.A., just like the first."

I do not know what first goads me into looking through the telescope—which is pointed directly at the Earth—perhaps I miss our brown planet more than I dare admit. Regardless, it is not so much a matter of 'why' but 'what'—for what I see through it is a world as green and fertile as any Earth of the past; a world as lush and emerald as the Red Planet herself—now terraformed to resemble the Earth of old—and whose dark side and light side are both visible (thanks to its position to Mars). And yet a world, too, that must ultimately not exist—for it occupies the same part of the sky where the brown Earth must of necessity be. A world, then, I suddenly realize, which is not *like* the Earth—but *is* the Earth. The Earth reborn. Impossibly, breathtakingly.

Beautifully, I think, feeling as though I might touch it, for here is our home as it once was, as it was meant to be: the clean, open fields, the mountains and hills, the seas and rivers—but also the cities and illuminated byways like glowing circuit boards. Also the—

I squint, adjusting the scope's aperture, compensating for glare. I want to see the lights, the intricate web of glitter—like back-lit dew on a leaf—the sparkle of sentience. The proof that Earth is a thinking thing, a dreaming thing, a thing perhaps without precedent.

But there is no proof, no intricate web of glitter, no illuminated byways like glowing circuits. There is only the planet's dark side and a perfect half-sphere of black—only one void against another and two impossible extremes—only the green of endless plant life and the unfathomable chasm of night.

In the end, only an Earth devoid of all human activity—as though we never even existed—and overrun by grass and vegetation. Overrun, I am now convinced, by the company's own super accelerant, M-4.

We hump for the next Oasis, double-timing it to beat the Captain—who we are now convinced has the Daze. (Why else would he not have told us? For surely he has known, receiving as he does updates from Mother, and thus Earth, regularly). The plan, meanwhile, such as it is, is simple: we will blast off in the medical rocket and rendezvous with Mother before hitching a ride back to Moon Plaza and applying for asylum—a long shot, to be sure, but more than we could hope for if the Captain finds out we entered one of the houses illegally. With luck, Crazy Cap will be mowing as he goes and so arrive well after us.

"*If* he's not there already," shouts Taylor as we run through the knee-high grass—referring to the medical rocket, playing Devil's Advocate. "And *if* the gnomes haven't gotten to it. They're getting bold, you know." He adds, looking at me: "Why the hell you packing that, anyway? Ain't *no* grass where we're going ..."

But I don't know why I'm packing 'that,' it—my light-trimmer—only that it feels necessary somehow, feels important, like it's the right thing to do, although I have no idea why.

And then we run, opting to save our breath, praying we get there before Cap, wondering what has become of our loved ones—hoping Moon Plaza will take us in.

The medical rocket is wasted—its consoles smashed, its stores emptied—to the extent that we have collapsed outside its open hatch in total exhaustion and despair. Worse, the air is filled with the roar of machinery—a roar with a bandsaw edge—one we know all too well for it is the sound of Cap's Big Track coming closer every second.

And then he has arrived, riding his tractor like a chariot, goading it forward into the clearing, motoring directly toward us until Taylor jumps up in a panic and sprints for the next bridge—his dark skin shining, his heels kicking up sod—as the Captain veers toward him suddenly and seems to gun the engine.

And then I am running, shouting at him to stop, as Taylor vanishes beneath the blades and the Big Track jounces, once, twice, the Captain laughing and throwing back his head, the iron tracks seeming to catch—until blood begins spewing like grass clippings from the mulch-vents and all I can hear is my friend screaming—gargling—dying beneath the Cap's iron beast.

That's when I realize it is *rotating*, swiveling, committing a zero-point turn so that the Oasis is sprinkled with entrails and the machine is pointed at me; at the center of the clearing—where I am wide open and vulnerable and will be mowed down no different than Taylor if I don't act and act quickly.

Then he accelerates and there is no time for anything—but to run. This I do, unhooking a plutonium sphere as I scuttle and dropping it into his path before diving suddenly to one side and rolling. Nor is it lost upon me that had I not retained the trimmer and fuel bandolier after the house I would surely be meeting the same fate as Taylor.

Instead there is a flash of light and a mighty explosion, and I am blasted no less than twenty feet—even as the Captain and his Big Trak are utterly obliterated.

And then I just watch: as the burning debris twirls down and the Oasis goes up in flames. As the medical rocket keels—and collapses into the fire.

I trim, heading due west, toward the next and perhaps final Oasis. Toward the next and perhaps final return rocket. As for *why* I do—I do not know, for the world of Man recedes further with each step—further, it seems, with each breath, and so, too, with each house left edged and ready for the mower.

All I know for certain is that this is what I do— what I have always done; and that, as a man, I was good at it. That I could channel my energy deftly and efficiently through the instrument so as to perform my duty smartly and surefootedly. And yet, that begs a question: What am I now, if no longer a man?

I'll tell you what I think. And that is that I have succumbed to the Daze, in no less a fashion than did the Captain or even Taylor when he ran for the bridge. Indeed, I cannot say beyond a certainty that any of this has even happened; or if it is rather, all of it, a kind of daydream, something experienced, perhaps exclusively, by those who toil long amongst the grass.

I trim—the blade of my instrument whirring pink and smooth through the stems—but grow weary; the foliage reaching higher the farther I push, my skin and hair and vision turning green, my thoughts turning outward—to the world, to the Formerly Red Planet, to Earth, and everything in them, every rock, every insect, every blade of grass.

CRASH DIVE

T-minus 15 and counting. All set there, Chief?

I look at my reflection in the cockpit's front window—the tired eyes, the premature wrinkles and crow's feet—and beyond: to the blue hole and return mirror—which will remain invisible to the naked eye until I am almost upon it.

Roger that. All systems are go and I am hot to drop.

Roger that, *Diver 7*. Nine and counting: 8 ... 7 ... 6 ...

I brace myself as the launch indicator switches from red to green—like a streetlight in the void—and the helmet's blue visor lowers ... locking into place.

2 ... 1 ...

I grip the Jesus handles.

Launch.

Elton John once sang, "And all this science, I don't understand. It's just my job five days a week." That's how it is when you're a Crash Diver: you don't need to understand blue holes or how they differ from wormholes and black holes or what a mobius mirror does—only that it *must* work, every time—because, at the end of the day, that isn't your job. Your job is to be a guinea pig: to be shot into the vortex at near light speed and experience what effect blue hole-assisted mirror travel has on the human body and psyche. Your job is to penetrate to whatever depth they've set the mirror—and, if you're lucky, to enter that mirror and get bounced back.

It hasn't always been like this. Before there was *Zebra Station*—with its luxurious gravity centrifuge and its row of black and yellow delta divers hanging like bats from the launch jib—there was *Blue One,* a sparsely-manned outpost which had sent the first human souls into the maw of the blue hole, men who had come back white-haired and emaciated, debilitated—mentally and physically—mad.

The Crash Diver Program changed all that. From now on only specially-trained pilots would be sent into the Hole, pilots who had the benefit of the first men's experiences as well as spacecraft designed specifically for the task. A lot was learned in a very short time—one of these things was that men who entered the vortex experienced a series of hallucinations, or Dive Visions, in which they briefly felt they had become someone or something else: a soldier in the Holy Roman Army, say, or a person of the opposite sex. Some even purported to have become animals or alien lifeforms—it was the latter which had apparently driven the men of *Blue One* clinically insane.

Another lesson was the fact that the farther a mirror was projected into the vortex the farther it could "cast" to its attendant portal; meaning the Hole might well hold the key to intergalactic space travel. This more than anything had accounted for the program's generous funding, not to mention its exhaustive launch table, which sometimes saw us drop as many as three times in a week. The chief problem, however, remained—and that was that the deeper one dropped, the more acute the hallucinations; hence, the missions had become increasingly volatile, increasingly dangerous.

Regardless, a decision had been made to make the next drop the deepest yet: all the way through the ergosphere—

right up to the outer event horizon. By which they meant right up to the point of no return, even by mirror refraction.

And I was the one who drew the unlucky straw.

It is raining. That's the first thing I notice, the first thing that tells me I am no longer in the cockpit. The second is that I'm bleeding—bleeding from the leg, which is making it difficult to press the attack. The third is that I'm dying—as is my opponent—dying beneath a blood red sky.

"It is finished," he says, stumbling forward and back—his blood flowing freely, his hair matted in sweat. "Look at you! Your broadsword is shattered. Your armor is compromised. Why is it you continue?"

But I do not know why I continue—only that I was a Crash Diver once and will be so again, and so must face the vision, endure its consequences. Endure them so that future generations may bridge the gulf of galaxies!

At last I say: "Are you better off? We die together, Sir Aglovere. Surely you—"

But I am baffled by my own voice, so familiar and yet strange, and by my own words, which have materialized from nowhere.

And then he is charging, hacking at me wildly, and I am forced back along the hedgerow: until I lose my footing over a protruding root and topple headlong into the mud and bramble—whereupon my opponent falls on what's left of my sword and is promptly run through, his entrails unspooling like loops of linked sausage and his eyes turning to empty glass.

At length he says, "We kill ourselves," and laughs, even as I push him off me.

And then we just lay there, staring at the sky, neither of us saying anything, as our blood pools together and spirals down the slope. As the clouds continue to rumble—pouring rain into our dying eyes.

The diver trembles violently as I shake the vision off.

... repeat, *Zebra One* to Diver 7, are you all right?

I feel my leg through my flight suit, half expecting it to be flayed wide open—but I am unharmed, of course.

Roger that, *Zebra One.* However I am experiencing turbulence I cannot account for—what can you tell me?

There is a long pause which is pregnant with static, after which *Zebra One* responds, choppily, Diver 7 ... *Zebra One.* Be advised ... some kind of anomaly. We are working ... before it effects the mirrors. Please ...

And then they are gone.

I am gone, too. At least, I am no longer in the cockpit. Instead, I awaken from a dream I cannot remember in a place I have never been—no, I can see now that is incorrect. I am *home,* still sequestered in the dingy sleeping quarters at the very back of the Temple—where I have remained now for three days without benefit of food or water, and where I shall stay—unto death, if necessary—until Rue Umbra shows me His face. Until He Who Created Everything bestows upon me the gift of His Holy visage.

"Master Hezekiah ... the Artifact is ready."

"Bring it to me, Jocasta. I will view it here in my chambers."

"Yes, Master."

I rise and swing my legs out of bed, and am startled briefly by my reflection in the bureau mirror. For it seems at first that I am someone—*something*—else; someone/something alien, with a gray, rumpled body and a face that is smooth like glass. Then it is gone and I see only myself: the green scales, the angled brow, the tired eyes of the High Priest of Samara.

At length Jocasta re-enters the room and places the box on the rug at my feet. "It is my hope—*our* hope, Master, the entire congregation's—that you will end your fast soon. May Rue Umbra light your way."

He moves to leave but hesitates, pausing in the doorway. "It is also hoped ... that you will be careful. This so-called Artifact—it is not of this world."

Then he is gone and I am alone with the box, the box containing the meteor which has somehow survived its entry into our atmosphere. The hollow meteor with the strange runes printed on its surface (at least, that is how it has been described to me). The thing whose existence is responsible for my crisis of faith.

Show me, Oh Highest One. Send me a sign. Reveal to me, your faithful servant, the naked face of God.

But Rue Umbra is silent as I open the box and lift out the Artifact, and proceed to examine it by the dim light of the candles. Nor is the object so unfathomable as I'd presumed: for it is clearly something designed to protect the head, similar in many respects to our Centurions' helmets (although charred and blackened from its journey through the atmosphere) and composed of materials I have never seen; some of which glow at the touch of my fingers and cause the Artifact to hum and to vibrate ...

Show me your face, Oh Lord, so that I may believe again!

But in the end there is nothing, only silence, as a glassy shield lowers smoothly and locks into place. As I stare into its curved, indigo-blue surface—which has become a kind of looking glass, a mirror—and see only myself, Hezekiah. Only the High Priest of Samara laid low by his fast.

Something is wrong. This much is clear as I stir from the vision and find the diver shaking—shaking as though it might fly apart any moment. *Zebra One,* meanwhile, is talking at me through my headset:

... get it back. We're trying ... but ... long shot. Repeat: we have ... return mirror. It's just ...

Again, damn you! You're breaking up. What about the mirror?

... has failed. We are trying—

But they are gone—and I am alone. Alone against the ergosphere, whose end must surely be near. Alone—in light of the mirror's failure— against the event horizon, beyond which lies Hell itself.

I pause, feeling it again. As though someone were in the cave with me, as though someone were watching.

I look to the mouth of the cavern, beyond which the snow continues to fall. No, it is nothing—the wind, perhaps, coursing through the opening.

I return to my work, continuing the stroke which will complete our leader (his snout blue with war paint, his shoulders broad and hairy), knowing he will be pleased. For I have captured him in truth—as well as the spirit of his hunt— captured him so that he might live for all time. And yet, as the winds moan and the torches falter, the feeling I am not alone persists, so that I again look to the door of the cave, and this time—someone is there.

The hominid doesn't move, doesn't seem to breathe, as I look at him, and for an instant I think, *Dr. Livingstone, I presume.* Then I laugh a little behind my visor, marveling that I can do so under the circumstances, and take a step forward, eliciting a growl from the creature I would not want to hear twice.

I hold, looking back at the diver—which is suspended nose-down in the middle of the air— before turning again to regard the creature and his art ... only to find them gone, replaced by a very old man in what appears to be a Tudor-style study parlor.

"Livingstone, Einstein, Hezekiah, we've been them all, at one time or another." He begins moving toward me, casually. "You are ... Diver 7. I presume."

I just look at him, saying nothing. Behind him is a blackboard which runs floor to ceiling and wall to wall, and is crowded with equations. Noticing my gaze, he says, "Ah, yes. Well. The hominid has his work, and I have mine."

He stops within a few feet of me, examining my flight suit. "Your helmet. You won't be needing it."

I look at him for what seems a long time. At last I reach up and trigger the visor, which glides up and out of the way, and take a deep breath. The air is fine.

"Where am I?" I ask, glancing about the room, noting its exotic décor: a red, cactus-like plant (without needles) which looks as though it belongs at the bottom of an alien sea; a black and silver obelisk the height of a man; a polished suit of armor standing sentinel in a corner. "And who are you?"

The old man smiles, warmly, compassionately. "I should have thought you'd have guessed. As for where, why, you're stone cold dead in the middle of a blue hole. Where else? The mirrors, alas, have failed—but you knew that already. No, what you really want to know is ... what does it all mean? The Hole, the visions, everything. Isn't that right, Diver 7?"

I look at the old man expectantly.

"Beats the hell out of me," he says, and moves toward the blackboard. "A blue hole is where mathematics go to die. No. What I have left is only conjecture, speculation—metaphysics rather than physics, notes as opposed to a complete script." He puts his hands on his hips, examining his formulas, and exhales, warily. "Of the trail of ink there is no end."

At length he begins moving again, pacing beyond the red plant and the black and silver obelisk, past the suit of armor which gleams like gold in the umber firelight. "Say, just say, for the sake of argument, that the Buddhists are right, and that reincarnation is real. And that its purpose is to evolve souls, to grow them—from the first spark of sentience to something approaching divinity. Would you allow that this was a worthy end to our travails?"

I don't say anything, only continue to watch him.

"Say, too, that these incarnations are infinite, or nearly so, occurring not just in this universe but a *multiverse,* so that, in time, we have experienced creation from every window and every door, every viewpoint—in short, we have been everyone and everything. *Mmm?* Shall we say it?"

He stops and turns around, begins pacing back toward me. "And that, as we reach the point of infinite progression, we begin to, slide, if you will, back and forth amongst our lifetimes—putting the lesson together, as it were, making of it a sphere, rather than a line, compressing everything into an infinitely dense mass, an Alpha and Omega, a singularity such as is found in the heart of our blue hole. Would you say then that we had solved the riddle of its phantasmagorias?"

He pauses not three feet away and I just look at him: the tired eyes, the deep wrinkles and crow's feet—at last, I understand.

I lift off my helmet.

"I was you, once," I say. "We were ... We will ..."

He nods, slowly. "Not only us but all men, all sentient beings. Nothing is wasted."

My mind reels. "But ... The Hole. My diver. It took those things to—"

He laughs suddenly. "Oh, that. Why, that's just a happy coincidence. You still don't understand, do you? You never needed the ship, or the vortex. You—we—were ready. Our infinite progression had reached—"

"Madness," I say. "Shadows within shadows."

But he is gone, replaced by Hezekiah. "It's the shadows that exist," he says, and I understand him perfectly in spite of his alien tongue. "The objects that create them; those are the illusions. Put another way: The ghost is real—the machine is not. Now—it is time."

And I am back in the cave, standing so close to the hominid I can smell him, watching him rub chalk on the stone, watching him create entire worlds. Until he looks at me sidelong and hands me the tool—thoughtfully, knowingly—as if he were encouraging me. As if he were saying: *You too can do it. You, too, are the Creator.*

Until I close my fingers on the chalk and everything fades to black.

And that blackness becomes Light.

I am become the White Fountain, the creator of worlds—the Big Bang which will expand outward, creating a new universe. Nor has the previous universe ceased to exist; for it dreams behind us on the other side of the Hole—its galaxies and star systems safely intact, its sentience growing by leaps and bounds.

Meanwhile, even amidst the crash and swirl of creation, I have remained—the godhead of an entirely new paradigm; the observer, and yet, somehow, the observed; the ghost in the rapidly expanding machine. Nor has every vestige of my former self been annihilated; for something has survived the explosion which even now hurtles outward into the maelstrom, spinning, tumbling, drifting ever further. For a billion years, it drifts, until, caught by a mid-size world's gravitational pull, it falls like a shooting star into an alien sea—a sea as red as blood—whereupon, again, it *drifts.*

Until it is retrieved from the water by a pair of eager hands—four-fingered hands—which grip the helmet firmly and place it into the boat, after which it is passed from one being to the other like the physical manifestation of a riddle, and finally put into a box.

Where it will remain—its secrets safe, its numeral '07' unseen—until delivered to the priest.

"What'd you think?" I asked the bouncer—a gargantuan brother named Pinky; I didn't ask—on the way out, even as the jukebox began to play and the room began to return to normal, meaning loud.

"Hmph," he hmphed, staring straight ahead, keeping an eye on the boys in the MAGA hats. "I think you're lucky to be getting out of here alive."

"That's live comedy," I said—a little dickishly, now that I remember it. "It's no country for snowflakes. This brother brings it."

Call it a manic response to the thrill of the kill—because that's precisely what I'd done, killed it—though not so manic that I didn't ask him for an escort to my car.

He lingered, seeming pensive, as I got in and started the engine—enough so that I rolled down my window and asked him, "You really didn't like it, did you?"

He shrugged his massive shoulders. "My job is to spot trouble and eliminate it. Not to stir it up. But I do think ... you said you were from New York?"

"I live there, that's right. Going home to visit family. Thought I'd line up some gigs along the way."

The man laughed a little. "That's right. You mentioned that in your routine. 'Haven't left my borough since those Mexicans flew them planes into the towers'—that was good."

I looked at him expectantly, wanting to know what it was he thought.

"Oh. It's just that ... Well, you should get out of New York more. See the country. Be good for your comedy."

I wasn't sure how to take that. "Yeah. Well. Keep an eye on those rednecks. At least until I'm down the road?"

He nodded as I put the car in gear. "There won't be any more trouble. That I can guarantee."

I gave him the Peace sign.

And then I was off—into the Kentucky night which sweated and lay silent across the fields. Into a damp fog which reminded me of New York—and was at the same time completely foreign.

It didn't take long to start comparing the bucolic beauty of the state by day, with its rolling horse farms and verdant, bluegrass pastures, with its indistinctiveness at night. It was like driving anywhere, even upstate New York (except for the complete lack of other vehicles and the plethora of Donald Trump campaign signs, which seemed to stand sentinel in every other field). To tell the truth, I was beginning to nod off when a headlight appeared in my rear-view mirror—just one, a motorcycle, maybe, or a car with a burned-out lamp—and began closing the distance between us. It's funny because I remember thinking distinctly that it was moving too fast—a cop, maybe—which bore out quickly as the little sun grew— resolving itself, at length, into the working headlamp of a dirty 4x4 pickup. A pickup now tailgating me at sixty-five miles-per-hour.

You got anything else to say, Lib-tard? Maybe you've got something to say about my girlfriend. Don't be shy. I'm sure we all want to hear it.

I thought that was your wingman.

Keep talking ...

There was a pronounced jolt as the bumper of the truck hit my car, hard enough that it skewed a little on the damp pavement, and my heart leapt into my throat. Jesus, was it possible? It had been two hours since that exchange, two hours and a junction, there was no way—

Again the bumpers collided, and again there was a jolt.

Tell her you're sorry.

The truck veered into the oncoming lane suddenly, accelerating, and I was forced to do likewise—I didn't want them beside me. Didn't want to know if they had weapons or not. Didn't want—

Who? Your service animal? Or its mother?

I floored it as the truck's battered quarter panel appeared outside my open window, hoping the little Camry's V6 would open up, hoping it had more power than it seemed. It did—and I launched forward, causing the front of the truck to slide back, and the scenery to blur past with dizzying speed. I recall slapping the steering wheel like a pimply kid in his first car. *Eat my dust, suckers! I'll see you in Hell!*

But the old pickup only roared forward like a rocket, instantly drawing alongside. That was the moment, of course. The moment I realized just how much trouble I was in. For what I saw outside my window was not just some car full of idiots. Rather, it was like something from a horror movie— *Duel,* maybe, of fucking *Birth of a Nation.* What I saw outside my window was a truck full of hooded men—like KKK members, only wearing brown instead of white—like scarecrows having sprung to life from the fields. Or executioners.

There were six of them in total, more than had been present in the bar (not that it mattered, they would have rounded up others, I was sure). The important thing is that it *was* them—

the MAGA crew—of that I had little doubt. Three of them were crowded into the cab while three others rode in the payload—all of them wearing crudely-stitched burlap hoods—and each brandishing some form of weapon, whether that meant a pistol or a rifle or a rusty pitchfork. The truck, meanwhile, was right out of central casting—I'd seen others like it in the red states I'd already passed through. You've seen them too: those jacked-up tanks with the huge tires and pig-ear smokestacks (their way of saying "fuck you" to the environmentalists), and the twin flags crackling in their payloads—usually an American and a "Don't Tread on Me," but sometimes a bona fide Confederate Southern cross, which is what this one had, along with one I couldn't clearly see. All I can say for certain is that the men in the back put down their weapons as I watched and appeared to fiddle with something in the payload—I really couldn't say because I had to look away in order to focus on the road.

Meanwhile it didn't exactly surprise me to see that I—we—were going about 90 miles-per-hour—the fastest I'd ever traveled in a moving vehicle, and a speed at which the Camry had become dangerously unstable. I thought then of my decision when I was young to never own a firearm, and laughed a little at my own expense. Only then (and how I'd managed to not think of it until that instant remains a mystery) did it finally occur to me: my bloody phone was right there on the passenger seat!

The truck's engine roared and its flags crackled as I snatched the thing up and dialed 911, putting it on speaker so that I might better focus on the road, not to mention re-grip the wheel firmly in both hands.

A moment later it came: "911, what's the address of your emergency?"

I stammered and babbled before managing, "Old State Route 51—yes—Old State Route 51, between Danville and Tomlinson. I'm being pursued by a truck full of masked men, h-heavily armed. Let me repeat that; they are heavily arm—"

"What is the make and model of the truck?"

I glanced out the window. "I—I don't know. A Ford, maybe. Yes, a Ford, I'm certain of it. It's dark green and has flags flying from the back. One of them's a Confederate. I—"

I noticed movement and focused on the man nearest me—by the window in the truck's passenger seat—saw him training his pistol on, on ...

My tire. My fucking front tire!

I let off the gas immediately and slowed down before veering into the lane behind them, even as the operator asked calmly, "Are you able to see the license number? If so, read it to me—as carefully as you can. Are they Kentucky plates?"

I was distracted by the men in the payload, who appeared to be lifting something heavy, but quickly focused on the plate. "Yes. Kentucky 527 CXS, Franklin County." I squinted in the fog. The lettering didn't look right. "I—I think it's been altered. I'm following as close as I dare, and it looks like—"

"You are behind them?"

"Yes. One of them was—"

"Sir, be advised that units are on the way and that you are not to pursue. Repeat, do not pursue. Pull over immediately and wait for officers to arrive. What is the make and model of your vehicle?"

"I—it's a blue Toyota—a Camry. 2004, I think. I'm—I'm slowing down. But so are they. There's men in the payload. It, it almost ..."

I was about to say that it looked like they were lifting, well, a trough, to be frank, one of those big aluminum vats used to water horses, when the men heave-hoed the thing twice ... and sent its contents hurling toward my windshield. At which point the thick, viscous stuff hit the glass like a hammer—exploding everywhere—and turned the world black.

Black and blood red.

I must have waited there on the shoulder of the road for an hour, at least, during which time I fetched a road flare from the trunk—the closest thing I had to a weapon, sadly—as well as the 5-gallon plastic gas can (which was full, like the Camry's tank, because the car's fuel gauge didn't work), although as to why I grabbed it I can't really say. Maybe I just wanted it close so I could refuel quickly if it became necessary. Maybe I already had some divination of an outcome—whether I was consciously aware of it or not.

What I *was* certain of is that no cops had shown up, nor whirred past through the fog with their lights flashing chaotically, in the entire time I'd been waiting. Likewise, my phone had remained silent—as if my call for help had simply fallen through the cracks, or never happened at all. One thing, for sure, *had* happened: a trough full of blood—animal blood, presumably—had been hurled at my windshield, and it had made one hell of a mess, a mess the worn wipers had been inadequate to clear, thus I'd had to clean the glass manually with wiper fluid and a towel.

I waited another five minutes before tentatively buckling my seatbelt and starting the car, peering down the road intensely, seeking any sign of the truck. It looked clear. Even the fog had lifted somewhat.

At last I edged onto the road, picking up speed gradually, using my blinker, which gave me a little laugh, increasing to 55 miles-per-hour. A portion of my act came unbidden to my mind—I was looking for what could have motivated them to murder, I suppose, beyond merely insulting someone's girlfriend—the Cavalcade of Clichés, I called it. It was the portion of the act where I'd recite, in rapid-fire succession, every bad joke anyone had ever told on a subject: in this case, Southerners. Rednecks.

What's the difference between Virginia and West Virginia? In Virginia, Moosehead is a beer. In West Virginia it's a misdemeanor.

How can you tell if a redneck is married? There are tobacco spit stains on both sides of his truck.

What can a pizza do that a redneck can't? Feed a family of four.

It was all pretty innocuous stuff, hardly anything to go to war over. And yet there had been a moment—just before my confrontation with the heckler—a moment that had struck me as strange, even by Bible Belt standards. It had occurred just after I'd segued into a semi-serious bit on Civil War monuments and social justice—a bit in which I'd gone so far as to defend the Antifa protestors who'd toppled the Silent Sam statue at Chapel Hill. I remembered it clearly because the room had fallen absolutely silent—so silent I heard the big bouncer—Pinky, God bless him—say, and I mean softly, "Move on."

Don't get me wrong. I was used to this sort of response when I challenged audience expectations. Indeed, had I been anywhere else—a college town, say—I would have been pontificating on the evils of political correctness—if for no other reason that when it comes to making an audience more malleable, a little cognitive dissonance can go a long way. But this felt as though I'd committed a real breach, had somehow touched on something I didn't and couldn't understand—and, moreover, had done so perhaps from a position of pure malice. Either way, the trouble had started almost immediately after, and, although I'd rebounded by show's end—some might even say spectacularly— with a flurry of region-specific crowd pleasers, I never got the sense that I'd been forgiven for what I'd said.

I listened in near silence as the radials droned against the surface of the road.

Or, Bright Boy—they were just a bunch of racist pieces of shit. I mean, surely that was possible, in the *fucking South?* Yes—even in 2019?

Forget it, I told myself, as the fog continued to lift and it became clear the truck was gone. It's over.

Whatever it had been.

It would be difficult to describe just how close they'd come to killing us all—how little time I'd had to yank the wheel and hit the brakes in those first awful seconds after they'd shot from the sideroad. All I know for certain is that I ended up facing in the opposite direction—even while they careened into the trees on the other side of the road ... where they quickly reversed, massive tires spinning, and narrowly missed me yet again—for I'd stepped on the gas and chirped out of their way.

And then we were right back where we'd started (only traveling in the opposite direction), piling down Old State Route 51 with our vehicles side by side and the truck's chrome stacks belching black smoke into the night. And I saw in the vespertine darkness what I couldn't have seen before—which was the flag previously blocked to me snapping and crackling in the wind. And I saw, too, that it was identical and yet radically different, for its colors were black, red, and green, and this filled me with a terror I could not define—in part because the combined colors felt alien and yet familiar, and in part because its very existence made of me an illiterate. Made me question if I knew anything beyond my borough in New York at all.

Not that I had time to dwell on it, for when next I glanced at the truck and its occupants I saw that the man in the passenger seat and the men in the payload had, all of them, pointed their firearms at me.

What I did next surprised even myself, for I sideswiped them without even thinking about it, and such was the impact that one of the men toppled from the payload and fell face-first into my window—where the whites of his eyes shown wide through the eyeholes of his hood—before he fell against the rushing pavement with a sickening slap-crunch and was instantly gone behind us. And then they were veering into *me*—although by intention or loss of control I couldn't possibly say—and I very nearly careened from the road—and yet, somehow, did not.

That was the moment, I think. The moment I knew what I was going to do. It was also the moment that the man in the truck's passenger seat shot clean through the door into my leg, spattering the upholstery with blood, and making me feel as if I might black out any second.

It's funny, because the gas can was in my hand and its lid taken off before I'd even consciously decided to grab it, nor did I hesitate before hurling it into the truck's cab and reaching for the road flare—which I quickly managed to uncap while driving and swipe against its striker. Then the Camry's interior filled with orange-white light and I threw the thing—threw it with everything I had, and before I even knew if I'd gotten it into the truck the Ford's cab exploded into something like the sun.

And then we were both skittering out of control, the burning truck toward the left shoulder and I toward the right, and the last thing I thought of before everything went black was how little things had changed in the fifty-two years I'd walked the planet. How little things had changed since Jesse Washington and Mary Turner and Emmett Till and James Chaney. Since Martin Luther King. Since 1981 and Michael Donald.

"Wake up, Yankee."

A voice in the blackness. A rich voice, a radio voice. A voice I had heard before.

"I'm not going to tell you again, New York. Wake up. I got something to tell you."

I opened my eyes, slowly, realizing my entire body had gone numb. The speaker's face swam into focus.

"I guess you're not feeling so smart now—are you?"

It would be hard to say what I noticed first, the fact that half his face was gone and that his brain was partially exposed, or that he was training a pistol on me, or that I knew him—had known him since before starting my act. All I know is that I recognized him immediately and that he was perfectly correct: I *didn't* feel very smart ... didn't feel much of anything now that the Camry and I were sort of one big casserole and the big bouncer was glaring at me from just outside my window.

"You—you *really* didn't like it, did you?" I gurgled—and laughed suddenly, causing a fit of convulsive coughing.

"Smart to the end, I guess," he said, and coughed a little himself, bringing up blood. I looked to where his head had been nearly cleaved in two. "What's gray and black and red all over?"

"Shut up and listen."

"Your brain," I said.

He jammed the muzzle of the gun against my forehead. "What's it feel like? Knowing you're going to where there ain't no God and there ain't no New York, just you and your Yankee friends, burning for what you did?"

I must have just looked at him.

"Knowing you pissed your life away telling jokes—while never once having stood for anything ... never once having sacrificed. What'd y'all think, that no negro served? That no negro ever died in that slaughter you called a war or bonded with his white brothers while defending his homeland?" He *hmphed,* something I found incredibly funny considering half his head was gone. "Maybe they didn't fight, but they were there—scouting, cooking, running supply—there when the battle against federal tyranny was joined, and there when it was lost. And they are here, now, in the bodies of their descendants—working as cops and dispatchers and magistrates; working as bouncers in roadside bars. And they will tolerate no more of the desecration of their ... Of their ..."

And then he was gone, just like that, the pistol tumbling and clattering against the ground, his body slumping unceremoniously out of sight. And it struck me that the 911 operator I had spoken to had almost certainly been one of them—not one of them in the truck, of course, but one of them in spirit—the unlikely sons of the confederacy. Or *something.*

And it struck me too that I would never know: no more than I would know why some people were convinced that Barack Obama or the U.N. or fucking Michael Moore were coming for their guns or that a global conspiracy of patriarchs ruled the world or that we were all being routinely poisoned by chem trails—people built mythologies, it was what they did, and more, was I any different? Hadn't I been equally convinced that a group of drunken Trump fans had decided to chase me down and kill me because they'd taken umbrage with my act?

You should get out of New York more. See the country. Be good for your comedy.

I laughed a little at that, tasting my own blood.

Get out of New York. Get out of our boroughs.

Oh vey.

Shouldn't we all.

"Meet you at the top!" Kerber hollered—cockily, as always—as he climbed rapidly past us. He gestured toward the cloud ceiling. "We'll leave a light on!"

Sean and Karen looked at each other as his balloon disappeared around the envelope of our own.

"Everything a competition," sighed Sean. There was a deafening roar as he toggled the blast valve. "Had to show us he could beat us on the ascent—even at night."

"Talk about that a little," I said, continuing to roll. "You mentioned that his balloon was different from yours. How so?" I nodded at Eddy, who moved the boom mic closer. "Just look out at the sky, Sean, not the camera."

He scratched at his beard and seemed to marshal his thoughts. "Well, he's running a gas balloon, not a hot-air vulcoon, which is what this is. A gas balloon uses gas instead of hot air for its lift, which is advantageous because you can stay up longer—a lot longer—and because it's so quiet. There's none of this," He toggled the blast valve again and there was a mighty roar as liquid propane vaporized and ignited. "So, on that level, they're extremely sought after. The problem is one of economy. Helium is *expensive.* Like, real expensive. Like five grand to fill a balloon expensive. So people use hydrogen—which, while relatively cheap, is also incredibly flammable. The *Hindenburg* was full of hydrogen, as is The *Excelsior.*"

He was referring, of course, to billionaire Ronald Trimp's promotional blimp—which, winds allowing, we'd be seeing when these balloons and others converged on the Super Bowl in the morning.

Sean looked at the camera awkwardly. "How was that?"

"That was good, Sean. Thanks." I stopped recording and ran the footage back—too far, to the point where the old Indian we'd encountered before takeoff was talking.

"They move," he said, gazing at the snow-smothered hills.

"T-they? The mountains? The mountains move?"

"Uh-huh. They fall from sky ... onto my land."

"Oh?"

He nodded. *"They move."*

I powered the camera down—there wouldn't be much to see until dawn, anyway—still thinking about his words. *They fall from the sky ... onto my land.*

"Wreckage from Jupiter 6?" prompted Eddy, noticing my expression. He was referring, of course, to the unmanned mission to the cloud planet, which had blown up in the earth's atmosphere immediately after its long journey home.

"Yeah. Maybe." I zippered my parka all the way up.

The two-way radio crackled to life. It was Kerber, calling from the other balloon. "West by northwest, you see that?"

It wasn't until Sean had turned on the spotlight and aimed it in that direction that what he was talking about became clear: for a kind of fog bank had rolled in seemingly out of nowhere—and was moving toward us at a shockingly rapid clip.

"Sean ... what is that?" I recall asking nervously.

But he didn't respond, at least not at first, and it took an elbow from Eddy to remind me why we were there in the first place.

I reactivated my camera. "Okay, folks. This is what reality TV's all about. Remember, we're not here."

I zoomed up on Sean's beard and focused as he toggled the mic.

"That's affirmative, *Gas Monkey,* we see it. Not sure we believe it, but we see it."

"The weather report said clear skies," cursed Karen, even as the radio crackled and Kerber came again: "It's nothing to worry about. A little thermal turbulence—*Gas Monkey* suggests letting it pass and carrying on."

I panned past Karen slowly enough to register her concerned expression before focusing on the approaching clouds, which bubbled and roiled and shown mauve-pink, like plumes of dry ice at a rock concert. Then they were upon us, reducing visibility dramatically and smelling faintly of ammonia.

"I'm not so sure," said Sean at last. Though I may have imagined it, it seemed there was a small quaver in his voice. *"Hot-air One* recommends seeing how thick it is before proceeding. Stand by."

"Negative, repeat negative on that. *Gas Monkey* will continue to ascend."

"Jesus Christ," hissed Sean, and released the mic.

I refocused on him, liking the way the purple fog rushed past him in the dark—

And something moved in that dark. Something like a giant scythe, which rose like a whale's pectoral fin breaching water and just as quickly vanished.

"Holy shit, what was that?" blurted Eddy, and jolted, his sudden movement rocking the basket.

Karen had seen it, too.

"Jesus, Sean, there's something out there ..."

"Something out—" He turned and looked into the mists, which bubbled and swirled, and I regained my senses enough to tape him as he did so.

"What'd it look like?" he asked, craning his neck to look up, then quickly cued his mic. *"Gas Monkey* this is *Hot-air One.* What's your altitude?"

"It wasn't them," said Karen.

"I repeat, *Hot-air One* to *Gas Monkey.* What is your present altitude?"

We all waited, shivering in the dark, and as we did so I zoomed up on Sean's face to capture his concern.

"It looked like a wing," Karen blurted suddenly.

He froze for a moment and didn't say anything. At last he looked from her to Eddy and then to me. "Ah. I see." He smiled suddenly and waved a finger. "You got me. Who's idea was it? *Hmmm,* let me guess ..." He looked back to Karen and was about to say something when there was a sound like a slab of meat hitting the concrete and he jolted abruptly and we all just froze, in part, I suppose, because we couldn't figure out what the massive, arrow-shaped thing that had suddenly materialized amongst us was. But then the blood dribbled from his mouth and Karen began screaming and I realized with horror that he'd in fact been impaled—impaled by some kind of spaded appendage, which uncurled in the mists even as I watched and was suddenly stretched taught—so that he was jerked from the basket with a sickening crunch and swung arms and legs akimbo into space.

That was the worst of it, I think, seeing him swung about like a ragdoll like that, and in such an empty void, his body rising and falling as though in slow-motion and his arms and legs flapping almost gracefully—even as the owner of that appendage passed through the beam of the spotlight and revealed itself in full.

In retrospect, I wish I'd continued recording, for what I saw in that instant is difficult to describe, even now. Suffice it to say that it had a body like that of a manta ray—upon who's tail the balloonist had been impaled—or a manta ray combined with a bat, albeit huge, and that it was covered with a kind of camouflage which reminded me of pictures I'd seen of Jupiter—just a roil of purples and pinks and browns. I suppose that was when it first hit me: the possibility that there might be a connection between this *thing* and the Jupiter 6 probe. That the probe might have brought something back, even if it had just been a sprinkling of microbes on its surface.

And then there was an explosion somewhere above us, the concussion of which rocked our balloon, and we all looked up to see *Gas Monkey*—my God, it was like the sun!—on fire; and yet that wasn't all we saw, for as it dropped it became evident that there were more of the bat/manta ray things attached, suckling it as it fell, crawling upon it like flies. Then it passed us like some kind of great meteor—its occupants shrieking and calling out—and was gone below, the heat of it still painting our faces, its awful smell, which was the smell of rotten eggs, filling our nostrils.

And then we were just drifting, all of us crouched low in the basket ... and the only sounds were those of Karen sobbing and my own pounding heart.

I'm not sure how much time passed, maybe five minutes, maybe twenty. All I know is that the sky had begun to lighten and that it was Eddy who spoke first, saying, "Hydrogen. They feed on hydrogen. We're safe."

I must have looked at him, because I remember clearly how pale he looked, how ill.

"Jupiter 6?" I said, although I already knew the answer.

"Why not?" He laughed a little to himself. "Cosmos. Carl Sagan. Hunters and floaters."

"Someone needs to toggle the propane," said Karen, absently, it seemed, as though she were a million miles away.

I looked at her to see a woman clearly in shock. "I'll do it. Okay? You—just relax." I looked at the apparatus for controlling the balloon. "The red lever?"

She nodded and sniffed, like a helpless little girl, and I climbed to my feet. Eddy grabbed my ankle.

"Wait. The cloud. Are we still in it?"

I scanned our surroundings. "Yes."

"Okay, toggle it and get back down. Quickly!"

I toggled it and got back down.

Quickly.

"What is it?" I asked.

"The cloud ... it's ... I think it's a form of camouflage. You know, like how octopuses squirt ink—but in this case it's to confuse their prey, not predators. Right? Okay. So that means as long as that cloud's there, we got trouble."

"But you said they—"

"Feed on hydrogen, that's right," he said. "But they don't *know* we're running on hot air—not yet."

"Which means—"

"Which means they're checking us out, right now."

I looked at the pink and purple clouds. "But wouldn't they have a way to, I don't know, *sense* when hydrogen is present?"

"I'm sure they do. Look, all I know is they just hit the jackpot with Kerber's gas balloon, and it looked a lot like ours, all right?"

"Right," I mumbled, seeing the truth of it. "And that's not our only problem."

"What do you mean?"

"I mean there's a giant meal called the *Excelsior* which could be hovering over the Super Bowl right now. Jesus. How many people does a stadium like that hold? 90,000? A hundred?"

No one said anything.

I climbed up and peeked over the basket's edge.

Sure enough, through a hole in the marmalade clouds, the stadium had come into view, shining like a north star and already crowded with balloons—including the *Excelsior*. I looked at the bullhorn in the corner of the basket, the one Sean had said he used to communicate with people on the ground. At least there was a way to warn the crowd—if and when we got there.

"The burner—it needs to be triggered again," said Karen, distantly. "And our altitude ... what is it?"

I looked at Eddy. The truth of it was, I was sort of hoping he'd take this one. But he only shook his head.

"Right," I sighed at last. "Okay. Is that the altimeter?" I gestured at the readout next to the burner valve.

Karen nodded.

"Okay—hold my beer."

And I counted to three.

What happened next happened very fast—so fast that I was unable to process the enormity of it until Eddy was long gone and so was most the floor, leaving us to dangle precariously as our feet sought the shattered plywood's edges and we hung onto the cold, chromed burner supports for life. For Karen had stood with me as I reached for the red propane valve (to check the altimeter herself, presumably) and thus been spared falling into nothing when one of the creature's knife-like tails penetrated the flooring—harpooning Eddy through his abdomen before jerking him clean through the plywood and dragging him screaming into the void.

But something else happened in that instant too, something which remains the single most terrifying aspect of the ordeal. For as we clung to the burner supports and tried to keep our feet on what was left of the floor, the head of one of the creatures darted from the fog—it was easily the size of a refrigerator laid on end—and just stopped: the tip of its nose all but touching my own and its huge eyes which were full of spirals regarding me with something like curiosity. Then it exhaled, blowing the hat off my head, and arced away into the mists, and as it went I felt a great rushing of wings as though a dozen others had suddenly abandoned their fascination with us and followed.

And then it was just us, Karen and I, gripping the burner supports and trying to keep our feet on what little remained to support them. And I knew that she knew we were safe now—at least from our Jovian hunters—but that we had a responsibility, too. For it was clear to both of us, I think, that the monsters had not merely lost interest but been *lured* away—by the promise of enough hydrogen to fill them all to bursting. By the promise of Ronald Trimp's leviathan blimp, which now loomed large in the slowly clearing mists.

By the time Karen had maneuvered us to a hard landing at the edge of the playing field, the first of the sword-tails were already circling the *Excelsior*—just circling and gliding, as though carefully sniffing the zeppelin out. As for myself, I knew we'd have but seconds before security responded— violently, I was sure—and so was scrambling with the bullhorn before the balloon's envelope had even fully deflated. I only remember that the thing was heavier and louder than I'd expected, and for the latter, at least, I was profoundly grateful.

"Ladies and gentlemen, I'm going to ask you all to get up and proceed to the nearest exits. Please don't panic, just do it now and in an orderly fashion."

But they did panic, almost instantly, probably because someone had already noticed the sword-tails, and the next thing I knew there was a sea of humanity crushing toward the exits even as the security staff ran at me across the field and the first explosion rocked the arena.

"Get on the ground!" I recall someone shouting in the instants before I was piledrived, and then I was literally seeing stars as the heavyset men piled on and at least one of them started kicking me in the ribs.

"Jesus, look up!" Karen shouted, and when I rolled over on my side I saw that she had leapt atop one of the men's backs and was forcibly lifting his head.

To the purple-pink sky and the soaring Jovian hunters. To the massive, dark-skinned zeppelin which was already on fire and continued to explode as additional cells were ignited.

And then I was free, they'd clambered off me at last, and I struggled for breath while still curled up on the Astroturf even as great chunks of burning wreckage began to reign down all around and Karen tried to help me to my feet. And yet even amidst all that it occurred to me: my camera might still be in the ruins of the balloon (for I'd placed it on a shelf below the bulwark right after the *Gas Monkey* had exploded). And the next thing I knew I was searching for and finding it and triggering the record button, pausing only to look at Karen over the viewfinder as she let go of my arms at last and began shaking her head.

"I—I've got a kid, if no longer a husband," she said, the tears streaming down her face. "I can't stay here."

"I know," I remember saying—as gently as I could under the circumstances. "Go. I'll be all right."

And then she smiled almost motherly—and was gone across the wreckage-littered field.

It didn't take long for what remained of the *Excelsior* to come crashing down, its great, bullet-shaped envelope almost completely burned away and its interior girders warping and melting. Nor did the hydrogen-eaters abandon it even then, but continued to draw sustenance from it as their abdominal sacs swelled and their manta ray/bat wings beat furiously and their eyes seemed to spiral like the storms of Jupiter itself.

As for myself, I'd retreated to the relative safety of a roofed area near the dugout, where I continued to record as the now-gorged hunters at last began to rise ... and in very short order disappeared into a cloud of their own making.

And then—finally—it was over, and I could only stare at the ruins of the *Excelsior* as a few survivors stumbled from the smoke and swirling particulate—at which instant I awakened as if from a dream and hurried to assist them.

I was helping an elderly woman get back on her feet when I first heard the gasps and expressions of surprise happening all around us. Nor did it take long to figure out what they were responding to, for when I followed their collective gaze to the blue-gray sky I saw two enormous creatures rising into the clouds—*huge* creatures, as big as mountains, shaking off avalanches of snow with each undulating breath, pulsing upward like man-of-wars in water.

And I remembered the old Indian.

They fall from sky ... onto my land.

And knew nothing would ever be the same.

DEATH GRADER

Statement of Ms. Eleanor "Elle" Westbrook (January 17th, 3:30 PM, interviewed by Detective Ollie Rowe)

Detective Rowe: I want you to relax, Ms. Westbrook—is it okay if I call you Eleanor?

Westbrook: I prefer Elle.

Detective Rowe: Elle. Now I want you to relax ... and tell me about the first time you saw the road grader actually move. Can you do that for me?

Westbrook: Sure. It was the day after Christmas—the 26th, I think. It was a Thursday. I remember it because, well, besides the grader moving for the first time, it was movie night in the community room. *Frozen II.* Which—

Detective Rowe: At Farmington Hall. The orphanage. Is that correct?

Westbrook: Yes, but—we don't call it that. An orphanage, that is. The nuns don't like it.

Detective Rowe: But you were home?

Westbrook: Yes. In my room. I'd had a terrible nightmare and was just waking up, when I heard—

Detective Rowe: Talk about that a little. Your nightmare. Do you remember it?

Westbrook: No. Not really. Just bits and pieces. I remember ...

Detective Rowe: Yes?

Westbrook: I remember ... it had the road grader in it. And it—it killed somebody. It ran over him with its front tires and then ...

Detective Rowe: Yes?

Westbrook: I'd rather not say.

Detective Rowe: But I'm asking you to, Elle. It's okay. It ran over him with its front tires and ...?

Westbrook: And then it dropped that big plow it has.

Detective Rowe: The moldboard. The blade it uses to grade the roads.

Westbrook: (inaudible)

Detective Rowe: I'm going to ask you to speak clearly and not just nod, okay? We're recording.

Westbrook: Yes, sir. That one. The big one. It—it dropped it right on him. And then I heard it strike the ground ... I mean, the pavement under the snow.

Detective Rowe: So it—look, I know how difficult this must be, considering ... So it passed clean through him, is that it?

Westbrook: (inaudible)

Detective Rowe: No nodding. Okay. What then?

Westbrook: He opened up. Like ... like a can of spaghetti.

Detective Rowe: (inaudible) Okay. I can see you're upset by this. Let's switch gears a bit. Did you recognize this—this man? You did say it was a he. Was it somebody you recognized from your real life? Your waking life?

Westbrook: No.

Detective Rowe: I see. And you're sure about that?

Westbrook: Yes. Positive. The grader was looking for someone to kill—when the man stumbled out of that bar on 4th Street, the one where all the homeless people hang out.

Detective Rowe: And where were you, in your dream, that is?

Westbrook: That's what's so funny. Because I distinctly remember watching the grader approach from the sidewalk, which was covered in snow. Just standing there, right outside the bar. And yet when I saw him killed I was inside the cab, looking down through the glass. At one point I was even way up above it—the grader, that is—like, like God. I guess I was sort of everywhere and nowhere, if that makes any sense.

Detective Rowe: Yes. Yes, it does. Okay. That's good. That's very good. Thank you. Let's go back now—to when you first saw it move. Is that all right?

Westbrook: Sure. Like I said, I'd just woken up from the dream when I heard it, just rumbling across the field where they'd been working on the road—

Detective Rowe: The I-890-North Schenectady Corridor.

Westbrook: Sure, I guess. So I went to my window—you know, to see what was going on, and saw it sputtering to a stop near the office trailers and other equipment—which were all covered in snow—just shutting down with a rattle, like it had been running for a long time. That's when I first noticed it, how clean it was—there was no snow on it at all. Like—

Detective Rowe: But it was there when you went to sleep, isn't that correct?

Westbrook: Yes, of course. Covered in snow. It hadn't moved since December, when they had that accident—you know, where the worker was killed.

Detective Rowe: Clarke. The foreman. I seem to recall they had several accidents; including when they rammed into that layer of concrete.

Westbrook: (inaudible)

Detective Rowe: What?

Westbrook: The Meyers. James and Mia. That's where the concrete was at. I used to talk with them sometimes, before the accid—

Detective Rowe: You knew them?

Westbrook: Before the traffic accident. The one with the semi. Last summer.

Detective Rowe: Yes, I seem to recall that too. Something about them accelerating out of control—

Westbrook: I think *they* did it.

Detective Rowe: I'm sorry?

Westbrook: The bugs.

Detective Rowe: The ... *bugs.*

Westbrook: (inaudible): In the concrete. Where the Meyers buried them. At least, until the road grader came along.

Detective Rowe: (inaudible) I want you to hold that, okay? Hold that very thought. There's a psychiatrist coming, Ms. Daniels, a very nice lady, who's going to talk with you about all that—when we're finished, okay?

Westbrook: Okay.

Detective Rowe: Now, and this is important, so I want you to think about it very carefully. Did you at any point see anyone get out of the motor grader?

Westbrook: You already asked me that.

Detective Rowe: Once more—for the record. Please.

Westbrook: No. Like I said.

Detective Rowe: But it *was* dark, isn't that right? Dark, and snowing.

Westbrook: Yes, but not like later. The storm was just getting started.

Detective Rowe: I see. And then you went back to—

Westbrook: No.

Detective Rowe: You didn't go back to sleep? What did you do?

Westbrook: I went down to the community room, to tell Sister Bryant.

Detective Rowe: All right. And ... were they still watching the movie ... (inaudible) *Frozen II?*

Westbrook: No. All the girls had gone to bed. It was just Sister Bryant, who had fallen asleep on the couch.

Detective Rowe: Okay. And did you wake her up, to tell her what you had seen?

Westbrook: (inaudible)

Detective Rowe: I'm sorry?

Westbrook: No. She ... she never liked me. So I thought it was a bad idea.

Detective Rowe: Oh. So there was—bad blood between you?

Westbrook: I wouldn't say that. I was fine with her. She just ... didn't like me. I didn't drive the road grader over her—if that's what you mean. That was them.

Detective Rowe: The, ah ... bugs?

Westbrook: Yeah. The ghosts of them. Their bodies are still in the cement.

Detective Rowe: I see. Okay. And then?

Westbrook: I waited for her to wake up.

Detective Rowe: All right. And?

Westbrook: Which took about an hour—I guess, maybe less—I was watching the news. Then she woke up ... and I told her all about it. About the machine.

Detective Rowe: About the grader. Okay. And what did she say?

Westbrook: She didn't believe me, not even for a second. So I led her to the window and we looked out, and sure enough, the snow had re-covered it—the entire road grader. It had even refilled its tracks.

Detective Rowe: I imagine that didn't go over so well.

Westbrook: No. And I got the switch for it. Which is why I didn't mention it again—to anybody—not even when the reports of people finding body parts in the snow started coming out. Of course I knew what was going on because I saw the grader leave every night—after which I would always dream it had killed someone. And then it would just rattle back and park itself, usually about 11 pm.

Detective Rowe: You were alone.

Westbrook: Yeah. But what's new.

Detective Rowe: And you knew something had to be done. At least that's what you told me earlier.

Westbrook: Sure—if I wasn't imaging everything.

Detective Rowe: And you decided you had to get closer. To inspect it yourself.

Westbrook: Yeah. The day after New Years. The day after they found the Smythe lady all chopped up in quarters.

Statement of Ms. Eleanor "Elle" Westbrook (January 17th, 5:30 PM, interviewed by Doctor Regina Daniels)

Dr. Daniels: So after you trudged through the snow and reached the road grader—and that must have been quite a task on January 2nd, when there was so much accumulation—you say you used a broom to clean off the moldboard—is that correct?

Westbrook: That big blade, yeah. That's when I noticed the blood—just splashed all over it like dried blackberry syrup. But there was something else, too, which was sort of draped over the plow like a garland, all shiny and pink.

Dr. Daniels: (inaudible) What on earth was it?

Westbrook: Oh, It was an intestine, though how it got on top of the plow I have no idea. All I know is I wanted to run away after that—as far away as I could, farther even than Farmington Hall—and would have ... if not for the voices.

Dr. Daniels: The voices. Coming from—where, exactly?

Westbrook: Oh, everywhere. And nowhere. Coming from my head. But also from the road grader—from its cab. Like there were people inside—little people, I thought, I don't know why—all talking at the same time. Like they were arguing.

Dr. Daniels: My goodness. Well. That must have been extremely frightening. What on earth did you do?

Westbrook: I wanted to run, like I said—

Dr. Daniels: Yes, I can see why—

Westbrook: But I didn't, because it seemed to be drawing me in, toward itself—the cab, that is. Like a big magnet. Not only that, but there was a weird light inside—not a bright light, like in a house, but sort of a fog, like those pictures you see of distant galaxies, just sort of a green smear. And the next thing I knew I had opened the hatch and climbed in and the door had slammed shut—which made me jump—and they started talking, just, addressing me directly, as plain and clear as you are now.

Dr. Daniels: Oh, my goodness ... And—and what did they say?

Westbrook: They—they told me that they needed my help. That they were getting too weak to move the grader but that their work wasn't finished and that much infestation remained. That if I helped them they would ... they would spare me. And then they began saying other things, most of which I didn't understand—only the tone, which was hateful. And then I did run, although I had difficulty with the door and banged my hand up real good.

Dr. Daniels: I *see* that.

Westbrook: But it didn't matter because I just had to get away. Because, you see, the whole terrible truth had become clear to me in that instant, clear by a kind of mind transfer, how the grader had cracked the concrete in which the aliens' ship was interred and freed their spirits—despite the Meyers' best effort to contain them—how its owner had been influenced to paint the thing black and write "Black Betty" on its frame (before later using it to run over his co-workers and finally to kill himself), even how they—the aliens, the bugs—had come to be here in the first place! And I couldn't take it— just couldn't take it—and ran through the snow straight back to Farmington, up to my bed, where I stayed all eve and most the next day, refusing to come down—even when they handed out the ice skates for our excursion the next night. Even when they picked the teams for the game at which Sister Bryant was—where Sister Bryant was, oh! Oh! (inaudible)

Dr. Daniels: *Shhh.* It's okay. Everything is okay. Let's just—I think that will be all for today. All right? You must be exhausted.

Westbrook: (inaudible) But it isn't okay. Because the fact is, Sister Bryant is dead. Worse, she's been ... oh, it's too horrible. And although you won't come out and say it ... you think I did it. Don't you?

Dr. Daniels: That's not for me to decide, Elle.

Westbrook: (inaudible) But you have decided— I can see it in your face. And not just for Sister Bryant ... but all of them. I wonder: has it ever occurred to you that I might have saved lives by doing what I did? That I might have even stopped the killing? (inaudible) No? Well, maybe you'll think about that the next time. Goodnight, Ms. Daniels.

Dr. Daniels: Goodnight, Elle. Try to sleep well.

Statement of Ms. Eleanor "Elle" Westbrook (January 18th, 3:30 PM, interviewed by Detective Ollie Rowe)

Detective Rowe: Okay. So. You say you had a plan from the instant you woke up—is that correct?

Westbrook: Yes, sir, since the moment Sister Bryant announced the hockey game—even though I pretended not to notice.

Detective Rowe: That would be the hockey game at Fenrow Park, next to Deep Lake—isn't that correct?

Westbrook: Yes, sir.

Detective Rowe: Which is why you returned to where the road grader was parked at on the eve of January 3rd, 2019, and proceeded to board it. Is that right?

Westbrook: Yes, that's right, at which time they began to speak to me just as before—the bugs, you understand—and told me to place my hands on the controls (the keys were still in it!), and that they would guide me from that point on—like a puppet, I suppose, or a marionette. For what they needed more than anything was my musculature, my bone and tendon, to drive the grader they had previously driven only with their minds. And I told them with my thoughts that I knew where many infestations could be killed all at once (for that's how they view us, as infestations, as a kind of cancer of the Earth; a *disease*) and we moved out, the black grader rattling and rumbling, belching plumes of smoke— its work lights winking on. Nor was it long before—

Detective Rowe: You came to Fenrow Park.

Westbrook: Yes. Because it's close to Farmington Hall. And I saw the lights almost immediately—the lights Sister Bryant had rented to light the game—and her, too, trudging through the snow toward the restrooms, bundled up like an Eskimo. And before I knew it the grader had accelerated toward her even though I tried to fight it and chased her all the way into the building, where it smashed into the masonry like a wrecking ball.

Detective Rowe: But she made it, did she not? Made it into the restrooms.

Westbrook: Oh, yes. Thank God. But then the gears started shifting and we were backing up—way up—not backing up and stopping, mind you, but backing up and launching forward again, circling around, so that we were parallel to the front of the building.

Detective Rowe: But, why? Why would you—why would they do that, Elle?

Westbrook: I didn't know! At least, not until the blade changed its orientation and became vertical—something I didn't even know it could do. Looking back I understand; it was going to shave off the front of the building. But then Sister Bryant stuck her head out (to see if it was clear, I suppose) and the gas pedal sunk to the floor, and we launched at her so fast that I didn't even realize what the bugs intended until the blade struck her neck and—and ...

Detective Rowe: And what, Elle? You must go on ...

Westbrook: And ... I don't want to. You know very well what happened after that.

Detective Rowe: I saw the aftermath, yes. If that's what you mean. But in fact, I don't know what happened; that's the point of all this. Now answer the question, please. What happened after the grader struck Sister Bryant?

Westbrook: (inaudible) I don't want ...

Detective Rowe: *What happened?*

Westbrook: She ... her ...

Detective Rowe: Tell me, you little monster! *What happened to Sister Bryant?*

Westbrook: *She was decapitated, okay?* The blade struck her in the neck and she was split like a cantaloupe and her head flew off and bounced off the blocks of the men's room and she ended up with blood all over her clean white habit and one eye staring up at us from the snow, okay? Are you happy now? Is that what you wanted to hear?

Detective Rowe: I want to hear the truth! I want to hear how a 15 year-old girl became a mass murderer over the course of mere weeks, and how she learned to drive that grader, even to expertly maneuver its—

Westbrook: I told you ... it was *them. The bugs.* They were behind everything, not just the grader but the car, too, that car that killed all those people just a few years ago, the black '66, the original Black Betty—the one owned by James Meyers and before that, a man named Crowley. They *bond* with machines, you understand, moving machines, just like they had a bond with their spacecraft, the one that came to Earth in 1966 and which is buried in the cement where the Meyers' house used to be—the one whose magnetic field might have destroyed the planet if they hadn't—

Detective Rowe: Enough! Admit it: You killed all those people and Sister Bryant too, and then you tried to kill the girls playing hockey, your own neighbors at Farmington, other orphans just like you. That's why you steered the grader toward the frozen lake ...

Westbrook: I *steered* it toward the lake precisely to avoid that, knowing it would break the ice before it ever reached them, knowing it would sink to the very bottom! And knowing, too, that without a machine to possess the bugs would simply dissipate, that they would scatter on the wind, never to endanger anyone again. And that's exactly what happened after the grader fell through, moaning like a keeled ship, groaning like a dinosaur—I know because I felt them, screaming and bickering amongst themselves, furious that they had misplayed their hands, their slimy, green, locust's hands!

Detective Rowe: I've heard enough. Just—just get her out of here.

(inaudible)

Detective Rowe: Just go, take her to the juvenile detention center. Hurry up.

(inaudible)

Detective Rowe: Sure. Send her on in.

(inaudible)

Dr. Daniels: Detective Rowe?

Detective Rowe: Yes, please, come on in. Have a seat.

Dr. Daniels: (inaudible) I take it that didn't go very well.

Detective Rowe: On the contrary, it went almost exactly as expected. Jesus. Just ...

Dr. Daniels: I'd try not to dwell on it. It'll make you crazy yourself. Besides (inaudible), I was told to give you this. Read it. It'll give you something to focus on.

Detective Rowe: It's the report on that chunk of concrete. The one at the demolished Meyers residence. Looks like they cracked it open, finally ... and ...

(inaudible)

Dr. Daniels: What?

Detective Rowe: I don't know ... looks like they found something—unusual. Something big. Something made out of ...

Dr. Daniels: What?

Detective Rowe: That's just it. They don't know.

Dr. Daniels: Isn't that strange?

Detective Rowe: Yeah. Yeah, it is.

Dr. Daniels: You look tired. How long has it been since you slept?

Detective Rowe: I don't even remember. (inaudible) What do you say, nightcap at Mortimer's?

Dr. Daniels: That sounds positively heavenly.

Detective Rowe: It does, doesn't it? Oh, and more thing.

Dr. Daniels: What? What is it?

Detective Rowe: You're closer than me: Turn off that fucking tape recorder.

Dr. Daniels: Oh, that. (inaudible) Don't mind if

The End

If you enjoyed this work of fiction, please consider
leaving a review at your point of sale. Thanks!

Wayne Kyle Spitzer is an American writer, illustrator, and filmmaker. He is the author of countless books, stories and other works, including a film (*Shadows in the Garden*), a screenplay (*Algernon Blackwood's The Willows*), and a memoir (*X-Ray Rider*). His work has appeared in *MetaStellar—Speculative fiction and beyond, subTerrain Magazine: Strong Words for a Polite Nation* and *Columbia: The Magazine of Northwest History,* among others. He holds a Master of Fine Arts degree from Eastern Washington University, a B.A. from Gonzaga University, and an A.A.S. from Spokane Falls Community College. His recent fiction includes *The Man/Woman War* cycle of stories as well as the *Dinosaur Apocalypse Saga*. He lives with his sweetheart Ngoc Trinh Ho in the Spokane Valley.